TENDER IS THE FLESH

AGUSTINA BAZTERRICA

WITH A NEW AFTERWORD BY THE AUTHOR

TRANSLATED FROM THE SPANISH BY

SARAH MOSES

PUSHKIN PRESS

Pushkin Press
Somerset House, Strand
London WC2R 1LA

Tender is the Flesh was first published as *Cadáver Exquisito* by Alfaguara in Argentina, 2017

First published by Pushkin Press in 2020
This edition first published in 2026

Work published within the framework of "Sur" Translation Support Program of the Ministry of Foreign Affairs and Worship of the Argentine Republic

Obra editada en el marco del Programa "Sur" de Apoyo a las Traducciones del Ministerio de Relaciones Exteriores y Culto de la República Argentina

ISBN 13: 978-1-80568-085-7

A CIP catalogue record for this title is available from the British Library

The authorised representative in the EEA is eucomply OÜ,
Pärnu mnt. 139b-14, 11317, Tallinn, Estonia,
hello@eucompliancepartner.com, +33757690241

Designed and typeset by Tetragon, London
Printed and bound in the United Kingdom by Clays Ltd, Elcograf S.p.A.

MIX
Paper | Supporting responsible forestry
FSC® C018072

www.pushkinpress.com

3 5 7 9 8 6 4 2

For my brother,
Gonzalo Bazterrica

What we see never lies in what we say.

GILLES DELEUZE

They nibble away at my brain,
Drinking the juice of my heart
And they tell me bedtime stories…

PATRICIO REY Y SUS REDONDITOS DE RICOTA

ONE

...and its expression was so human
that it filled me with horror...

LEOPOLDO LUGONES

1

Carcass. Cut in half. Stunner. Slaughter line. Spray wash. These words appear in his head and strike him. Destroy him. But they're not just words. They're the blood, the dense smell, the automation, the absence of thought. They burst in on the night, catch him off guard. When he wakes, his body is covered in a film of sweat because he knows that what awaits is another day of slaughtering humans.

No one calls them that, he thinks, as he lights a cigarette. He doesn't call them that when he has to explain the meat cycle to a new employee. They could arrest him for it, even send him to the Municipal Slaughterhouse and process him. Assassinate him, would be the correct term, but it can't be used. While he removes his soaked shirt, he tries to clear the persistent idea that this is what they are: humans bred as animals for consumption. He goes to the refrigerator and pours himself cold water. He drinks it slowly. His brain warns him that there are words that cover up the world.

There are words that are convenient, hygienic. Legal.

He opens the window; the heat is suffocating. He stands there smoking and breathes the still night air. With cows and pigs it was easy. It was a trade he'd learnt at the Cypress, the meat processing plant he'd inherited from his father. True, the screams of a pig being skinned could petrify you, but hearing protectors were used and eventually it became just one more sound. Now that he's the boss's right-hand man, he has to monitor and train the new employees. Teaching to kill is worse than killing. He sticks his head out the window. Breathes the thick air, it burns.

He wishes he could anaesthetize himself and live without feeling anything. Act automatically, observe, breathe and nothing more. See everything, understand and not talk. But the memories are there, they remain with him.

Many people have naturalized what the media insist on calling the "Transition". But he hasn't because he knows that transition is a word that doesn't convey how quick and ruthless the process was. One word to sum up and classify the unfathomable. An empty word. Change, transformation, shift: synonyms that appear to mean the same thing, though the choice of one over the other speaks to a distinct view of the world. They've all naturalized cannibalism, he thinks. Cannibalism, another word that could cause him major problems.

He remembers when they announced the existence of GGB. The mass hysteria, the suicides, the fear. After GGB, animals could no longer be eaten because they'd been infected by a virus that was fatal to humans. That was the official line. The words carry the weight necessary to mould us, to suppress all questioning, he thinks.

Barefoot, he walks through the house. After GGB, the world changed definitively. They tried vaccines, antidotes, but the virus resisted and mutated. He remembers articles that spoke of the revenge of the vegans, others about acts of violence against animals, doctors on television explaining what to do about the lack of protein, journalists confirming that there wasn't yet a cure for the animal virus. He sighs and lights another cigarette.

He's alone. His wife has gone to live with her mother. It's not that he still misses her, but there's an emptiness in the house that keeps him awake, that troubles him. He takes a book off the shelf. No longer tired, he turns on the light to read, then turns it off. He touches the scar on his hand. The incident happened a long time ago and it doesn't hurt any more. It was a pig. He was very young, just starting out and hadn't known that the meat needed to be respected until the meat bit him and almost took his hand off. The foreman and the others couldn't stop laughing. You've been baptized, they said. His father didn't say anything. After that bite, they stopped seeing him as the boss's son and he became one of the team. But neither the team nor the Cypress Processing Plant exist, he thinks.

He picks up his phone. There are three missed calls from his mother-in-law. None from his wife.

Unable to bear the heat, he decides to shower. He turns on the tap and sticks his head under the cold water. He wants to erase the distant images, the memories that persist. The piles of cats and dogs burned alive. A scratch meant death. The smell of burned meat lingered for weeks. He remembers the groups in yellow protective suits that scoured the neighbourhoods at night, killing and burning every animal that crossed their paths.

The cold water falls onto his back. He sits down on the floor of the shower and slowly shakes his head. But he can't stop remembering. Groups of people had started killing others and eating them in secret. The press documented a case of two unemployed Bolivians who had been attacked, dismembered and barbecued by a group of neighbours. When he read the news, he shuddered. It was the first public scandal of its kind and instilled the idea in society that in the end, meat is meat, it doesn't matter where it's from.

He tilts his head up so the water falls onto his face. What he wants is for the drops to wipe his mind blank. But he knows the memories are there, they always will be. In some countries, immigrants began to disappear en masse. Immigrants, the marginalized, the poor. They were persecuted and eventually slaughtered. Legalization occurred when the governments gave in to pressure from a big-money industry that had come to a halt. They adapted the processing plants and regulations. Not long after, they began to breed people as animals to supply the massive demand for meat.

He gets out of the shower and barely dries himself off. In the mirror, he sees there are bags under his eyes. He believes in a theory that some people have tried to talk about. But those who have done so publicly have been silenced. The most eminent zoologist, whose articles claimed the virus was a lie, had an opportune accident. He thinks it was all staged to reduce overpopulation. For as long as he can recall, there's been talk of the scarcity of resources. He remembers the riots in countries like China, where people killed each other as a result of overcrowding, though none of the media outlets reported the news from this angle. The person who said that the world was going to explode was his father: "The planet is going to burst at any minute. You'll see, Son, it's either going to be blown to bits or all of us are going to die from some plague. Look at what's happening in China, they've already started killing themselves because there's so many people, there's no room for them all. And here, there's still room here, but we're running out of water, food, air. Everything's going to hell." He'd looked at his father almost with pity because he'd thought he was just an old man rambling on. But now he knows his father had been right.

The purge had resulted in other benefits: the population and poverty had been reduced, and there was meat. Prices were high, but the market was growing at an accelerated rate. There were massive protests, hunger strikes, complaints filed by human rights organizations, and at the same time, articles, research and news stories that had an impact on public opinion. Prestigious universities claimed that animal protein was necessary to live, doctors confirmed that plant protein didn't contain all the essential amino acids, experts assured that gas emissions had been reduced, but malnutrition was on the rise, magazines published articles on the dark side of vegetables. The protest centres began to disperse and the media went on reporting cases of people they said had died of the animal virus.

The heat continues to suffocate him. He walks to the porch naked. The air is still. He lies down in the hammock and tries to sleep. A commercial plays again and again in his mind. A woman who's beautiful but dressed conservatively is putting dinner on the table for her three children and husband. She looks at the camera and says: "I serve my family special food, it's the same meat as always, but tastier." The whole family smiles and eats their dinner.

The government, his government, decided to resignify the product. They gave human meat the name "special meat". Instead of just "meat", now there's "special tenderloin", "special cutlets", "special kidneys".

He doesn't call it special meat. He uses technical words to refer to what is a human but will never be a person, to what is always a product. To the number of heads to be processed, to the lot waiting in the unloading yard, to the slaughter line that must run in a constant and orderly manner, to the excrement that needs to be sold for manure, to the offal sector. No one can call them humans because that would mean giving them an identity. They call them product, or meat, or food. Except for him, he would prefer not to have to call them by any name.

2

The road to the tannery always seems long to him. It's a dirt road that runs straight, past kilometres and kilometres of empty fields. Once there were cows, sheep, horses. Now there isn't anything, not that can be seen with the naked eye.

His phone rings. He pulls over and answers the call. It's his mother-in-law, and he tells her he can't talk because he's on the road. She speaks in a low voice, in a whisper. She tells him that Cecilia is doing better, but that she needs more time, she's not ready to move back yet. He doesn't say anything and she hangs up.

The tannery oppresses him. It's the smell of waste water full of hair, earth, oil, blood, refuse, fat and chemicals. And it's Señor Urami.

The desolate landscape forces him to remember, to question, yet again, why he's still in this line of work. He was only at the Cypress for a year after he'd finished secondary school. Then he decided to study veterinary science. His father had approved and been happy about it. But not long after, the animal virus became an epidemic. He moved back home because his father had lost his mind. The doctors diagnosed him with senile dementia, but he knows his father couldn't handle the Transition. Many people suffered an acute depression and gave up on life, others dissociated themselves from reality, some simply committed suicide.

He sees the sign, "Hifu Tannery. 3 km". Señor Urami, the tannery's Japanese owner, despises the world in general and loves skin in particular.

As he drives along the deserted road, he slowly shakes his head because he doesn't want to remember. But he does. His father talking about the books that watched over him at night, his father accusing the neighbours of being hitmen, his father dancing with his dead wife, his father lost in the fields in his underwear, singing the national anthem to a tree, his father in a nursing home, the processing plant sold to pay off the debt and keep the house, his father's absent gaze to this day, when he visits.

He enters the tannery and feels something strike him in the chest. It's the smell of the chemicals that halt the process of skin decomposition. It's a smell that chokes him. The employees work in complete silence. At first glance, it seems almost transcendental, a Zen-like silence, but it's Señor Urami, who's observing them from up in his office. Not only does he watch the employees and monitor their work, he has cameras all over the tannery.

He goes up to Señor Urami's office. There's never a wait. Invariably two Japanese secretaries greet him and serve him red tea in a transparent mug, not bothering to ask if he'd like any. He thinks that Señor Urami doesn't look at people, and instead measures them. The owner of the tannery is always smiling and he feels that when this man observes him, what he's really doing is calculating how many metres of skin he can remove in one piece if he slaughters him, flays him and removes his flesh on the spot.

The office is simple, sleek, but on the wall hangs a cheap reproduction of Michelangelo's *The Last Judgement*. He's seen the print many times, but it's only today that he notices the person holding flayed skin. Señor Urami observes him, sees the disconcerted look on his face and, guessing his thoughts, says that the man is Saint Bartholomew, a martyr who was flayed to death, that it's a colourful detail, doesn't he think. He nods but doesn't say a word because he thinks it's an unnecessary detail.

Señor Urami talks, recites, as though he were revealing a series of indisputable truths to a large audience. His lips glisten with saliva; they're the lips of a fish, or a toad. There's a dampness to him, a zigzag to his movements. There's something eel-like about Señor Urami. All he can do is look at the owner of the tannery in silence, because essentially, it's the same speech every time. He thinks that Señor Urami needs to reaffirm reality through words, as though words created and maintain the world in which he lives. This he imagines in silence, while the walls of the office slowly begin to disappear, the floor dissolves and the Japanese secretaries vanish into the air, evaporate. All of this he sees because it's what he wants, but it'll never happen because Señor Urami is talking about numbers, about the new chemicals and dyes being tested at the tannery, and telling him, as though he didn't already know it, how difficult it is now with this product, that he misses working with cow skin. Although, he clarifies, human skin is the smoothest in nature because it has the finest grain. He picks up the phone and says something in Japanese. One of the secretaries comes in with a huge folder. Señor

Urami opens it and displays samples of different types of skins. He touches them as though they were ceremonial objects, explaining how to avoid defects when the lot is wounded in transit, which happens because human skin is more delicate. This is the first time Señor Urami has shown him the folder. He looks at the samples of skins that have been placed in front of him, but doesn't touch them. With his finger, Señor Urami points to a very white sample with marks on it. He says it's one of the most valuable skins, though a large percentage had to be discarded because there were deep wounds. He repeats that he's only able to conceal superficial wounds. Señor Urami says that this folder was put together especially for him, so he could show it to the people at the processing plant and breeding centre, and it would be clear which skins they have to be most careful with. Señor Urami stands up, gets a printout from a drawer, hands it to him and says that he's already sent off the new design, though it still has to be perfected because of the importance of the cut at the moment of flaying, since a poorly made cut means metres of leather wasted, and the cut needs to be symmetrical. Señor Urami picks up the phone again. A secretary comes in with a transparent teapot. He gestures to the secretary and she serves more tea. Señor Urami continues to talk to him with words that are measured, harmonious. He picks up the mug, takes a sip, though he doesn't want any. Señor Urami's words construct a small, controlled world that's full of cracks. A world that could fracture with one inappropriate word. He talks about the essential importance of the flaying machine, how if it's not calibrated correctly it can rip the skin, of how the fresh skin he's sent from the processing plant requires further refrigeration so that subsequent flesh removal is not as cumbersome, of the need for the lots to be well hydrated so the skin doesn't dry out and crack, of having to talk to the people at the breeding centre about this because they're not following the liquid diet, of how stunning needs to be carried out with precision because if the product is slaughtered carelessly, it'll show on the skin, which gets tough and is more difficult to work with because, he points out, "Everything is reflected in the skin, it's the largest organ in the body." His smile never fading, Señor Urami exaggerates the pronunciation of this sentence in Spanish, and with it, ends his speech, following it with a measured silence.

He knows he doesn't have to say anything to this man, just agree, but there are words that strike at his brain, accumulate, cause damage. He wishes he could say atrocity, inclemency, excess, sadism to Señor Urami. He wishes these words could rip open the man's smile, perforate the regulated silence, compress the air until it chokes them.

But he remains silent and smiles.

Señor Urami never accompanies him out, but this time they walk downstairs together. Before he leaves, Señor Urami stops him next to a tank of whitewash to monitor an employee handling skins that are still covered in hair. They must be from a breeding centre, he thinks, because the skins from the processing plant are completely hairless. Señor Urami makes a gesture. The manager appears and proceeds to yell at a worker who's removing the flesh from a fresh skin. It seems he's doing a poor job. To justify the employee's apparent inefficiency, the manager tries to explain to Señor Urami that the fleshing machine's roller is broken and that they're not used to manual flesh removal. Señor Urami interrupts him with another gesture. The manager bows and leaves.

Then they walk to the tanning drum. Señor Urami stops and tells him he wants black skins. Out of nowhere, with no explanation. He lies and says that a lot will be arriving shortly. Señor Urami nods and says goodbye.

Whenever he leaves the building, he needs a cigarette. Inevitably an employee comes over to tell him horrific things about Señor Urami. Rumour has it he assassinated and flayed people before the Transition, that the walls of his house are covered in human skin, that he keeps people in his basement and that it gives him great pleasure to flay them alive. He doesn't understand why the employees tell him these things. All of it's possible, he thinks, but the only thing he knows for certain is that Señor Urami runs his business with a reign of terror and that it works.

He leaves the tannery and feels relief. But then he questions, yet again, why he exposes himself to this. The answer is always the same. He knows why he does this work. Because he's the best and they pay him accordingly, because he doesn't know how to do anything else and because his father's health depends on it.

There are times when one has to bear the weight of the world.

3

The processing plant does business with several breeding centres, but he only includes those that provide the greatest quantity of heads on the meat circuit. Guerrero Iraola used to be one of them, but the quality of their product declined. They started sending lots with violent heads, and the more violent a head is the more difficult it is to stun. He was at Tod Voldelig to finalize the initial operation, but this is the first time he's included the breeding centre on the meat run.

Before going in, he calls his father's nursing home. A woman named Nélida answers. Nélida truly doesn't care about the things she's in charge of, and she exaggerates this with a passion. Her voice is nervy, but beneath it he senses a tiredness that erodes her, consumes her. She tells him that his father, whom she calls Don Armando, is doing fine. He tells Nélida he'll stop by for a visit soon, that he's already transferred the money for this month. Nélida calls him "dear", says, "Don't worry, dear, Don Armando is stable, he has his moments, but he's stable."

He asks her if by "moments" she means episodes. She tells him not to worry, it's nothing they can't handle.

The call ends and he sits in the car for a few minutes. He looks for his sister's number, is about to call her, but then he changes his mind.

He enters the breeding centre. El Gringo, the owner of Tod Voldelig, apologizes, says he's with a man from Germany who wants to buy a large lot, tells him he has to show this man around, explain the business to him, because the German is new and doesn't understand a thing, he just stopped by out of nowhere. El Gringo wasn't able to let him know. Not a problem, he says, he'll join them.

El Gringo is clumsy. He moves as though the air were too thick for him. Unable to gauge the magnitude of his body, he bumps into people, into things. He sweats. A lot.

When he met El Gringo, he thought it was a mistake to work with his breeding centre, but he's efficient and one of the few who were able to resolve a number of problems with the lots. His is the sort of intelligence that doesn't need refinement.

El Gringo introduces him to the man from Germany. Egmont Schrei. They shake hands. Egmont doesn't look him in the eye. He's wearing jeans that appear brand new, a shirt that's too clean. White sneakers. He looks out of place with his ironed shirt, his blond hair plastered to his skull. But he knows this. Egmont doesn't say a word, because he knows it, and his clothes, which only a foreigner who's never set foot in the fields would wear, serve to place him at the exact distance he needs to negotiate the deal.

He sees El Gringo take out an automatic translator, a device he's familiar with, though he's never had reason to use one. He's never been abroad. It's an old model, he can tell because there are only three or four languages. El Gringo talks into the machine and it automatically translates everything into German. The machine tells Egmont that he'll be taken around the breeding centre, that they'll start with the teasing stud. Egmont nods and doesn't show his hands, which are behind his back.

They walk through rows of covered cages. El Gringo tells Egmont that a breeding centre is a great living warehouse of meat, and he raises his arms as though he were handing him the key to the business. Egmont doesn't appear to understand. El Gringo abandons the grandiloquent definitions and moves on to the basics, explaining how he keeps the heads separate, each in its own cage, to avoid violent outbursts, and so they don't injure or eat one another. The device translates into the mechanical voice of a woman.

He sees Egmont nod and can't help but think of the irony. The meat that eats meat.

El Gringo opens the stud's cage. The straw on the floor looks fresh and there are two metal bins secured to the bars. One contains water. The other, which is empty, is for feed. El Gringo speaks into the device and explains that he raised the teasing stud from when he was just a little thing, that he's First Generation Pure. The German looks at the stud with curiosity. He takes out his automatic translator, a new model. He asks what "generation pure" is. El Gringo explains that FGPs are heads born and bred in captivity. They haven't been genetically modified or given injections to accelerate their growth. Egmont appears to understand and doesn't comment. El Gringo picks up where he left off, with a topic he seems to find more interesting, and explains that studs are purchased for their genetic quality. This one's a teaser stud, he says, because even though he's not castrated, and he tries to inseminate the females and mounts them, he's not used for breeding. El Gringo tells the German that he calls the stud a teaser because he detects the females that are ready for fertilization. The other studs are the ones destined to fill tin cans with semen that will then be collected for artificial insemination. The device translates.

Egmont wants to go into the cage, but stops himself. The stud moves, looks at him, and he takes a step back. El Gringo doesn't realize how uncomfortable the German is so he keeps talking, says that studs are purchased according to the feed conversion ratio and the quality of their musculature, but he's proud not to have bought this one; he raised him, he clarifies for the second time. He explains how artificial insemination is fundamental in order to avoid disease and how it enables the production of more homogeneous lots for the processing plants, among many other benefits. El Gringo winks at the German and finishes off by saying, "It's only worth the investment if you're dealing with more than a hundred heads because we're talking a lot of money for maintenance and specialized staff."

The German speaks into the device and asks why they use the teaser stud since these are not pigs nor are they horses, they're humans, and why does the stud mount the females, he wants to know, he shouldn't be allowed to, he says, it's hardly hygienic. A man's voice translates. It sounds more natural than the woman's voice.

El Gringo laughs a little uncomfortably. No one calls them humans, not here, not where it's prohibited. "No, of course they're not pigs, though genetically they're quite similar. But they don't carry the virus." Then it's silent; the voice on the machine cracks. El Gringo looks it over. He hits it a little and it starts. "This male is capable of detecting when a female is in silent heat and he leaves her in optimal condition for me. We realized that when the stud mounts a female, she's more willing to be inseminated. But he's had a vasectomy so he can't impregnate her; we've got to have genetic control. In any case, he's examined regularly. He's clean and vaccinated."

He sees the way the space fills with El Gringo's words. They're light words, they weigh nothing. They're words he feels mix with others that are incomprehensible, the mechanical words spoken by an artificial voice, a voice that doesn't know that all these words can conceal him, even suffocate him.

The German looks silently at the stud and there's something like envy or admiration in his eyes. He laughs and says, "This guy doesn't lead too bad a life." The machine translates. El Gringo looks at Egmont with surprise and laughs to hide the mix of irritation and disgust he feels.

As he watches El Gringo respond to Egmont, he sees the way questions arise and get clogged in the man's brain: How is Egmont capable of comparing himself to a head? How could he want to be one of them, an animal? After a long and uncomfortable silence, El Gringo answers, "It's short-lived, when the stud's of no more use, he's sent to the processing plant like the rest."

El Gringo keeps talking as though there were no other option. The owner of Tod Voldelig is nervous, beads of sweat slide down his forehead and are held up, just barely, in the pits of his face. Egmont asks if the heads talk. He's surprised it's so quiet. El Gringo tells him they're isolated in incubators from when they're little, and later on in cages. He says their vocal cords are removed so they're easier to control. "No one wants them to talk because meat doesn't talk," he says. "They do communicate, but with simplified language. We know if they're cold, hot, the basics."

The stud scratches a testicle. On his forehead, an interlocking "T" and "V" have been branded with hot iron. He's naked, like all the heads in all the breeding centres. His gaze is opaque, as though behind the impossibility of uttering words madness lurks.

"Next year, I'll be showing him at the Rural Society," El Gringo says in a triumphant voice, and he laughs and it sounds like a rat scratching at a wall. Egmont looks at him without understanding and El Gringo explains that the Rural Society gives prizes for the best heads from the purest races.

They walk past the cages. El Gringo steps away from Egmont and approaches him, just as he's thinking there must be more than 200 in the barn. And it's not the only barn. The man puts a hand on his shoulder. The hand is heavy. He feels the heat, the sweat, coming off this hand that's starting to dampen his shirt. In a low voice, El Gringo says, "Tejo, listen, I'll send the new lot over next week. Premium meat, export quality. I'll throw in a few FGPs."

He feels El Gringo's wheezing breath next to his ear. "Last month you sent us a lot with two sick heads. The Food Standards Agency didn't authorize packaging. We had to throw them to the Scavengers. Krieg told me to tell you that if it happens again, he'll take his business elsewhere."

El Gringo nods. "I'll finish up with Egmont and we'll discuss it," he says, and leads them to his office.

There are no Japanese secretaries and no red tea. There's barely any space in the room and the walls are made of fibreboard. This is what he's thinking when El Gringo hands him a brochure and says, "Here, Tejo, read this," before explaining to Egmont that he's exporting blood from a special lot of impregnated females. He clarifies that the blood has special properties. The brochure's large red letters say that the procedure reduces the number of unproductive hours of the merchandise.

He thinks: merchandise, another word that obscures the world.

El Gringo is still talking. He clarifies that the uses of blood from pregnant females are infinite. He says that in the past the blood business wasn't exploited because it was illegal. And that he gets paid a fortune because when blood is drawn from a female, inevitably she ends up aborting after becoming anaemic. The machine translates. The words fall onto the table with a weight that's disconcerting. El Gringo tells Egmont that this is a business worth investing in.

Egmont doesn't say anything. Neither of them does. El Gringo dries his forehead with the sleeve of his shirt. They leave the office.

They pass the dairy-head sector. Machines are suctioning the females' udders, that's what El Gringo calls them, and into the device, he says, "The milk from these udders is top-quality." El Gringo offers them both a glass, which only Egmont accepts, and says, "Recently milked." He explains that these females are skittish and have a short productive life. They get stressed easily and when they're no longer of use, their meat has to be sent to the processing plant that supplies the fast food industry, that way he can maximize profit. The German nods and says, "*Sehr schmackhaft,*" and the machine translates, "Very tasty".

On the way to the exit, they pass the barn where the impregnated females are kept. Some are in cages, others lie on tables. They have no arms or legs.

He looks away. He knows that at many breeding centres it's common practice to maim the impregnated females who otherwise would kill their fetuses by ramming their stomachs against the bars of their cage, or by not eating, by doing whatever it takes to prevent their babies from being born and dying in a processing plant. If only they knew, he thinks.

El Gringo quickens his step and says things to Egmont, who doesn't see the impregnated females on the tables.

The adjoining barn houses the kids in their incubators. The German stops to look at the machines. He takes pictures.

"Tejo," El Gringo says, approaching him, his sticky sweat giving off a sickly odour. "What you told me about the FSA is concerning. I'll give the specialists another call tomorrow and have them come in to examine the heads. If you get one that needs to be discarded, let me know and I'll discount it."

The specialists studied medicine, he thinks, but when their job is to examine the lots at breeding centres, no one calls them doctors.

"Another thing, Gringo, you'll have to stop skimping on transport lorries. The other day two arrived half-dead."

El Gringo nods.

"No one expects them to travel first class, but don't pile them up like bags of flour because they faint, or hit their heads, and if they die, who pays? And also, they get injured and then the tanneries pay less for the leather. The boss isn't happy about this either."

He gives El Gringo the folder of samples from Señor Urami. "You'll have to be especially careful with the lightest skins. I'll leave this folder with you for a few weeks so you can take a good look at the value of each sample, and treat the most expensive skins with extra care."

El Gringo goes red. "Point taken, it won't happen again. A truck broke down and I piled them up a little more than usual to get the order in."

They walk through another barn. El Gringo opens one of the cages. He takes out a female with a rope around her neck.

He opens her mouth. She looks cold, is trembling.

"Look at this set of teeth. Perfectly healthy," El Gringo says. He raises her arms and opens her legs. Egmont moves closer to take a look. El Gringo speaks into the machine: "It's important to invest in vaccines and medication to keep them healthy. A lot of antibiotics. All of my heads have their papers up to date and in order."

The German looks at her closely. He walks around, crouches down, looks at her feet, spreads her toes. He speaks into the device, which translates, "Is she one of the purified generation?"

El Gringo suppresses a smile. "No, she's not Generation Pure. She's been genetically modified to grow a lot faster, and we complement that with special food and injections."

"But does that change her flavour?"

"Her meat is quite tasty. Of course, FGP is upper-grade meat, but the quality of this meat is excellent."

He sees El Gringo take out a device that looks like a tube. It's one he's familiar with—they use it at the processing plant. El Gringo places one end of the tube on the female's arm. He presses a button and she opens her mouth in pain. It leaves a wound no bigger than a millimetre on her arm, but it bleeds. El Gringo gestures to an employee who approaches to dress the wound.

Inside the tube there's a piece of meat from the female's arm. It's stretched out and very small, no bigger than half a finger. El Gringo hands it to the German and tells him to give it a try. The German hesitates. But after a few seconds, he tries it and smiles.

"Quite tasty, isn't it? And what you've got there is a solid hunk of protein," El Gringo says into the machine, which translates.

The German nods.

"This is prime-grade meat, Tejo," El Gringo says in a low voice, approaching him.

"If you send us a head or two with tough meat, I can cover for you; the boss knows the stunners can slip up when they strike, but there's no screwing around with the FSA."

"Right, of course."

"They used to accept bribes when it was pigs and cows, but today, forget about it. You have to understand that they're all paranoid because of the virus. They'll file a claim against you and shut down your plant."

El Gringo nods. He takes the rope and puts the female in the cage. She loses her balance and falls into the hay.

The smell of barbecue is in the air. They go to the rest area, where the farmhands are roasting a rack of meat on a cross. El Gringo explains to Egmont that they've been preparing it since eight in the morning, "So it melts in your mouth," and that the guys are actually about to eat a kid. "It's the most tender kind of meat, there's only just a little, because a kid doesn't weigh as much as a calf. We're celebrating because one of them became a father," he explains. "Want a sandwich?"

Egmont nods, but he says no and the other two look at him with surprise. No one turns down this meat, eating it could cost a month's salary. El Gringo doesn't say anything because he knows that his sales depend on the quantity of heads the Krieg Processing Plant buys. One of the farmhands cuts off a piece of kid meat and makes two sandwiches. He adds a spicy sauce that's reddish-orange in colour.

They walk to a small barn. El Gringo opens another cage and motions to them to come over. He says into the machine: "I've started breeding obese heads. I overfeed them so that later I can sell them to a processing plant that specializes in fat. They make everything, even gourmet crackers."

The German distances himself a little to eat his sandwich. He does this bent over, not wanting to stain his clothes. The sauce falls very close to his sneakers. El Gringo goes over to give him a handkerchief, but Egmont gestures to show he's fine, that the sandwich is good; he stands there eating.

"Gringo, I need black skin."

"I'm actually just negotiating to have a lot brought over from Africa, Tejo. You're not the first to put in a request."

"I'll confirm the number of heads later."

"Apparently some famous designer is making clothes with black leather now and demand is going to skyrocket this winter."

It's time for him to leave. He can't handle El Gringo's voice any longer. He can't bear the way the man's words accumulate in the air.

They pass a white barn that's new, that he didn't see on his way in. El Gringo points to it and talks into the machine, saying that he's investing in another business and is going to breed heads for organ transplantation. Egmont moves closer and seems interested. El Gringo takes a bite of his sandwich, and with his mouth full of meat says, "They finally passed the law. It'll require more licences and inspections, but it's more profitable. Another good business to invest in."

He doesn't care to hear any more of El Gringo's words and says goodbye. The German is about to shake his hand, but stops himself when he sees there's oil from the sandwich on it. He makes a gesture of apology and under his breath says, "*Entschuldigung,*" and then smiles. The machine doesn't translate.

From the corner of his mouth, the orange sauce slowly falls and begins to drip onto his white sneakers.

4

He gets up early because he has to stop by the butcher shops. His wife is still at her mother's place.

He goes into a room that's empty except for a cot in its centre. He touches the cot's white wood. On the headboard, there's a drawing of a bear and a duck hugging. They're surrounded by squirrels and butterflies and trees and a smiling sun. There are no clouds or humans. It had been his cot and then it was his son's. Products with sweet innocent animals on them are no longer sold. They've been replaced by little boats, dainty flowers, fairies, gnomes. He knows he has to get rid of it, to destroy and burn it before his wife comes back. But he can't.

He's drinking *mate* when he hears the horn of a truck at the entrance to his house. It startles him and he drops the *mate* and burns himself. He goes up to the window and sees the red Tod Voldelig letters.

His house is fairly isolated. The closest neighbours are two kilometres away. To get to it, you have to open the gate, which he thought he'd locked, and follow the road furrowed on both sides by eucalyptus trees. He's surprised he didn't hear the truck's motor or see the cloud of dust. He used to have dogs that would chase after cars and bark at them. Their absence left a silence that's oppressive, complete.

Someone is clapping and calling his name. "Hello, Señor Tejo?"

"Yes, that's me."

"I've got a gift from El Gringo. Can you sign here?"

He signs without thinking. The man hands him an envelope and then walks over to the truck. He opens the back door, goes in and takes out a female.

"What is that?"

"It's a female FGP."

"Take her back, okay? Now."

The man stands there not knowing what to do, and looks at him, confused. No one would turn down a gift like this. The sale of the female would amount to a small fortune. The man tugs on the rope around her neck because he doesn't know what to do. The female moves submissively.

"I can't. If I take her back, El Gringo will get rid of me."

The man tightens the rope and holds out the other end. But he doesn't reach for it, and the man throws the rope to the ground, takes a few quick steps, gets into the truck and drives off.

5

"Gringo, what did you send me?"

"A gift."

"I kill heads, I don't breed them, okay?"

"Just keep her for a few days and then we'll have ourselves a barbecue."

"I don't have the time nor means to keep her for a few days. I don't want her."

"I'll send the men over tomorrow to slaughter her for you."

"If I want to slaughter her, I'll do it myself."

"Then it's settled. I sent you all the papers in case you want to sell her. She's healthy, all her vaccines are up to date. You can also cross-breed her. She's at just the right age for reproducing. But most important is that she's an FGP."

He doesn't answer. El Gringo tells him that this female is a luxury, repeats that she's got pure genes, as if he didn't know it, and says that she's from a consignment that's been given almond-based feed for over a year now. "It's for a demanding client who orders custom-raised meat," he explains, and says that he breeds a few extra heads in case any die. El Gringo says goodbye, but first he clarifies that the gift is intended as recognition of how much he values doing business with the Krieg Processing Plant.

"Right, thank you," he says and hangs up in a rage. In his mind, he curses El Gringo and his gift. He sits down and looks at the time. It's getting late. He goes out to untie the female from the tree where he left her. She hasn't taken the rope off her neck. Of course, he thinks, she doesn't know she can. He moves towards her and she begins to tremble. She looks at the ground. Urinates. He takes her to the barn and ties her to the door of a broken and rusted truck.

He goes into the house and thinks about what he can leave her to eat. El Gringo didn't send any balanced feed; all he sent was a problem. He opens the fridge. One lemon. Three beers. Two tomatoes. Half a cucumber. And a pot of leftovers from some meal, which he smells and decides is still good. It's white rice.

He takes a bowl of water and another full of cold rice out to the barn. Then he locks the door and leaves.

6

The toughest part of the meat run is the butcher shops because he has to go into the city, because he has to see Spanel, because the heat of the concrete makes it hard to breathe, because he has to respect the curfew, because the buildings and the plazas and the streets remind him that there were once more people, a lot more.

Before the Transition, the butcher shops were staffed by poorly paid employees. They were often forced by the owners to adulterate the meat so it could be sold after it had begun to rot. When he worked at his father's processing plant, one employee told him: "What we sell is dead, it's rotting and apparently people don't want to accept that." Between sips of *mate*, the man told him the secrets to adulterating meat so it looks fresh and doesn't smell: "For packaged meat, we use carbon monoxide, the meat on display needs a lot of cold, bleach, sodium bicarbonate, vinegar and seasoning, a lot of pepper." People always confessed things to him. He thinks it's because he's a good listener and isn't interested in talking about himself. The employee explained that his boss would make up for losses by buying meat that had been confiscated by the FSA, carcasses full of worms, and that he'd have to work the meat and then put it on sale. He explained that "working the meat" meant leaving it in the fridge for a long time so the cold would get rid of the smell. He said that his boss forced him to sell diseased meat covered in yellow spots, which he'd had to remove. The employee wanted to leave, to get a job at the Cypress Processing Plant since it had such a good reputation. He just wanted to do honest work so he could support his family. He couldn't take the smell of bleach, the stench of rotting chicken made him vomit, he'd never felt so sick and miserable. And he couldn't look the customers in the eye, the women who were trying to make ends meet, and asked for whatever was cheapest to make breaded *milanesas* for their children. If his boss wasn't there, he gave them whatever was freshest; otherwise he had to sell them the rotten meat, and afterwards he couldn't sleep because of the guilt. This job was consuming him little by little. The employee told him all this and he talked to his father, who decided to stop selling meat to the butcher shop and hire the man to come and work for him.

His father is a person of integrity, that's why he went crazy.

He gets into his car and sighs. But right away he remembers he's going to see Spanel and smiles, though seeing her is always complicated.

While he's driving, an image bursts into his mind. It's the female in his barn. What is she doing? Does she have enough food? Is she cold? He has these thoughts and silently curses El Gringo.

He arrives at Spanel Butchers and gets out of the car. The city's pavements are cleaner now that there are no dogs. And emptier.

In the city, everything is extreme. Raging.

After the Transition, the butcher shops closed down and it was only later, once cannibalism had been legitimized, that some of them reopened. The new shops are exclusive and run by their owners, who demand extremely high-quality products. Few are able to open a second location, and those who do have a relative or someone they can absolutely trust run it.

The special meat sold at butcher shops isn't affordable, which is why there's a black market, to sell a cheaper product that doesn't need to be inspected or vaccinated, that's easy meat, with a first and last name. That's what illegal meat is called, meat obtained and produced after the curfew. But it'll also never be genetically modified and monitored to make it more tender, tasty and addictive.

Spanel was one of the first to reopen her butcher shop. He knows she's indifferent to the world. The only thing she can do is slice meat and she does this with the coolness of a surgeon. The viscous energy, the cold air in which smells are suspended, the white tiles intended to affirm hygiene, the apron stained with blood, it's all the same to her. For Spanel, touching, chopping, grinding, processing, deboning, cutting up what was once breathing, is an automatic task, but it's one done with precision. Hers is a passion that's contained, calculated.

With special meat it was necessary to adapt to new cuts, new measures and weights, new tastes. Spanel was the first and the quickest to do so because she handled meat with chilling detachment. Initially, she only had a few customers: the maids of the rich. But she had an eye for business and opened the first shop in the neighbourhood with the greatest purchasing power. The maids picked up the meat, disgusted and confused, and always clarified that they'd been sent by the man or woman they worked for, as if doing so were necessary. Spanel looked at these women with a grimace, but it was one of understanding, and the maids always came back for more, with increasing confidence, until finally they stopped giving explanations. Over time, the customers became more frequent. The fact that a woman ran the shop put everyone at ease.

But none of them knows what this woman thinks. Except for him. He knows her well because she used to work at his father's processing plant.

Spanel says strange things to him while she smokes. He wants the visit to be over with as soon as possible because her frozen intensity makes him uneasy. And Spanel keeps him there—she does it every time—just like when he started working at his father's plant and she brought him to the cutting room after everyone had left.

He thinks she doesn't have anyone to talk to, anyone to share her thoughts with. He also believes that Spanel would be willing to lie down on the cutting table again and that she'd be just as efficient and distant as she'd been when he wasn't yet a man. Or not. Now she'd be vulnerable and fragile, opening her eyes so that he could enter, there, beyond the cold.

She has an assistant, a man he's never known to say a word. The assistant does the drudge work; he loads the carcasses into the cold storage room and cleans the shop. His gaze is like a dog's, full of unconditional loyalty and contained ferocity. He doesn't know the assistant's name, since Spanel never addresses the man, and when he's at the shop, "El Perro", the dog, generally makes himself scarce.

At first Spanel copied the traditional cuts of beef so the change wouldn't be as abrupt. A customer would walk in and it was like being in a butcher shop of times past. Over the years, the shop transformed, gradually but persistently. First it was the packaged hands that Spanel placed off to the side where they were hidden among the *milanesas* à la provençale, the cuts of tri-tip and the kidneys. The label read "Special Meat", but on another part of the package, Spanel clarified that it was "Upper Extremity", strategically avoiding the word hand. Then she added packaged feet, which were displayed on a bed of lettuce with the label "Lower Extremity", and later on, a platter with tongues, penises, noses, testicles and a sign that said "Spanel's Delicacies".

Before long, people began to ask for front or hind trotters, using the cuts of pork to refer to upper and lower extremities. The industry took this as permission and started to label products with these euphemisms that nullified all horror.

Today Spanel sells brochettes made of ears and fingers, which she calls "mixed brochettes". She sells eyeball liquor. And tongue à la vinaigrette.

She leads him to a room at the back of the shop with a wooden table and two chairs. They're surrounded by fridges that hold the half carcasses she takes out of the cold storage room to slice and then sell. The human torso is referred to as a "carcass". The possibility of calling it a "half torso" isn't contemplated. In the fridges, there are also arms and legs.

Spanel asks him to take a seat and serves him a glass of foot-pressed wine. He drinks the wine because he needs it, so he can look her in the eye, so he doesn't remember the way she pushed him onto the table that was usually covered in cow entrails, but then was as clean as an operating table, and lowered his trousers without saying a word. The way she lifted her apron, which was still stained with blood, climbed onto the table where he lay naked and carefully lowered herself, grabbing hold of the hooks used to move the cows.

It's not that he thinks Spanel is dangerous, or crazy, or that he pictures her naked (because he's never seen her naked), or that he's only ever met a few female butchers and that all of them have been inscrutable, impossible to decipher. It's that he also needs the wine so he can listen to her calmly, because her words drive at his brain. They're frigid, stabbing words, like when she said "no" and grabbed his arms and held them against the table forcefully, after he'd tried to touch her, take off her apron, run his fingers through her hair. Or when he went up to her the next day and the only thing she said was "goodbye", with no explanation, no kiss on her way out. Later he learnt that she'd inherited a small fortune, which was how she'd bought the butcher shop.

He hands her forms to sign that certify her interaction with the Krieg Processing Plant and state that she doesn't adulterate the meat. These are formalities because it's known that no one does, not now, not with special meat.

Spanel signs the forms and takes a sip of wine. It's ten in the morning.

She offers him a cigarette and lights it for him. While they smoke, she says, "I don't get why a person's smile is considered attractive. When someone smiles, they're showing their skeleton." He realizes he's never seen her smile, not even when she took hold of the hooks, raised her face and cried out in pleasure. It was a single cry, a cry both brutal and dark.

"I know that when I die somebody's going to sell my flesh on the black market, one of my awful distant relatives. That's why I smoke and drink, so I taste bitter and no one gets any pleasure out of my death." She takes a quick drag and says, "Today I'm the butcher, tomorrow I might be the cattle." He downs his wine and tells her he doesn't understand, she has money and can ensure she's not eaten when she dies, a lot of people do. She gives him a look that could be pity: "No one can be sure of anything. Let them eat me, I'll give them horrible indigestion." She opens her mouth, without showing her teeth, and lets out a guttural sound that could be a cackle, but isn't. "I'm surrounded by death, all day long, at all hours of the day," she says, and points to the carcasses in the fridges. "Everything indicates that my destiny is in there. Or do you think we won't have to pay for this?"

"Then why don't you give it up? Why not sell the shop and do something else?"

She looks at him and takes a long drag. For a while she doesn't say anything, as though the answer were obvious and didn't need words. Then she exhales the smoke slowly and says, "Who knows, maybe one day I'll sell your ribs at a good price. But not before I try one."

He drinks some more wine and says, "You'd better, no doubt I'm delicious," and gives her a big smile, showing off his skeleton. She looks at him with icy eyes. He knows she's serious. And that this conversation is prohibited, that these words could cause major problems for them. But he needs someone to say what no one does.

The shop's doorbell rings. A customer. Spanel leaves him to take care of business.

El Perro appears and, without looking at him, gets a half carcass out of the fridge and takes it to a cold room with a glass door. He can see everything El Perro does. The man hangs the half carcass so it doesn't get contaminated. He removes the NMSA approval labels and begins to butcher the meat. He makes a fine cut over the ribs to remove a good piece of skirt steak.

While he's watching El Perro, he thinks that he no longer knows the cuts of meat off by heart. During the adaptation process, many of the names of bovine cuts were carried over and mixed with those for pork. New directories were written up and posters were redesigned to show the cuts of special meat. The posters are never shown to the public. El Perro takes a saw and cuts the nape of the neck.

Spanel comes in and serves more wine. She sits down and says that people are starting to order brains again. A doctor had confirmed that eating brains caused who-knows-what disease, one with some compound name, but now apparently other doctors and several universities have confirmed that's not the case. She knows that viscous mass can't be good for you if it's not inside your head. But she'll buy them and cut them into slices. It's tough to do, she says, because they're quite slippery. She asks him if he can put in this week's order for her, but doesn't wait for his answer. She picks up a pen and begins to write. He doesn't clarify that she can order online. He likes to watch Spanel write: she's silent, concentrating, serious.

He looks at her closely while she finishes the order, the letters she writes squeezed tight together. Spanel has a detained beauty about her. It disturbs him that there's something feminine beneath the brutal aura she takes great care to give off. There's something admirable in her artificial indifference.

There's something about her he'd like to break.

7

After the Transition, he'd always spend the night in the city, in a hotel, whenever he was on the meat run, and then the following day he'd go to the game reserve. That way he saved a few hours on the road. But with the female in his barn, he has to go back home.

Before leaving the city, he buys balanced feed specially formulated for domestic heads.

When he gets home, it's night. He leaves the car and goes straight to the barn, cursing El Gringo. It had to be right now, right in the middle of the week he's on the meat run that El Gringo unloads this problem on him. Right when Cecilia isn't around.

He opens the barn. The female is curled up on the floor, in the fetal position. She's asleep and looks cold despite the heat. The rice and water are gone. He prods her a little with his foot and she jumps. She protects her head and curls up further.

He goes into the house and gets some old blankets, which he brings back to the barn and places next to the female. Then he picks up the bowls, fills them and returns with them to the barn. He sits down on a bale of hay and looks at her. She crouches over one of the bowls and slowly drinks some water.

She never looks at him. Her life is fear, he thinks.

He knows he can raise her, that it's permitted. He's aware

there are people who do so, and who eat their domestic heads alive, part by part. They say the meat tastes better, claim it's really fresh. Tutorials are available that explain how, when and where to make the cuts so the product doesn't die early.

Owning slaves is prohibited. He remembers the allegations against a family that was later prosecuted for keeping ten female slaves in a clandestine workshop. They were branded. The family had bought them from a breeding centre and trained them. They'd all been taken to the Municipal Slaughterhouse. The females and the family became special meat. The press reported on the case for weeks. He remembers there was a sentence that everyone repeated, horrified: "Slavery is barbaric."

She's no one and she's in my barn, he thinks.

He doesn't know what to do with the female. She's dirty. He'll have to wash her at some point.

He closes the door to the barn and goes over to the house. Inside, he takes off his clothes and steps into the shower. He could sell her and get rid of the problem. He could raise her, inseminate her, start with a small lot of heads, branch off from the processing plant. He could escape, leave everything, abandon his father, his wife, his dead child, the cot waiting to be destroyed.

8

Nélida's call wakes him up. "Don Armando had a breakdown, dear. Nothing serious, but I thought you should know. I don't need you to come in, though it would be nice. You know your father's happy to see you, even if he doesn't always recognize you. Whenever you visit, there are no episodes for a few days afterwards."

He thanks her for letting him know and says he'll stop by at some point. He hangs up and lies in bed thinking he doesn't want the day to begin.

Once he's put the kettle on the stove, he gets dressed. While he takes the first sip of *mate*, he calls the game reserve. He explains that he has a family emergency, says he'll call back to reschedule the visit. Then he calls Krieg and tells him that he'll need more time for the meat run. Krieg says that he can take as long as he needs, but that he's waiting for him to interview two job applicants.

After thinking it over for a few seconds, he calls his sister. He tells her that their father is doing fine and that she should visit him. She says she's busy, raising two kids and running the house takes up all her free time, but she'll go soon. It's harder for her to get to the nursing home from the city, she says, it's so far away and she's afraid about getting back after curfew. She says this with contempt, as though the world were to blame for her choices. Then she changes her tone of voice and tells him that they haven't seen each other in forever, says she wants to have him and Cecilia over for dinner and asks how she's doing, whether she's still staying with her mother. He says he'll call back at some point and hangs up.

He opens the door to the barn. The female is lying on the blankets. She wakes with a start. He picks up the bowls and returns with water and balanced feed. Then he sees she's found a spot to relieve herself. When he gets back, he'll have to clean it up, he thinks tiredly. He hardly looks at her because she's a nuisance, this naked woman in his barn.

Once he's in his car he drives straight to the nursing home. He never lets Nélida know ahead of time when he's coming. It's the best and most expensive facility in the area that he's paying for, and he feels it's his right to show up unannounced.

The nursing home is located between his house and the city. It's in a residential area of gated communities. Whenever he goes to visit his father, he makes a stop a few kilometres before the home.

He parks and walks towards the entrance to the abandoned zoo. The chains that locked the gate are broken. The grass overgrown, the cages empty.

Going to the zoo is risky because there are still animals loose. He knows this, and he doesn't care. The mass killings took place in the cities, but for a long time, there were people who clung to their pets, unwilling to kill them. It's said that some of these people were killed by the virus. Others abandoned their dogs, cats, horses out in the country, in the middle of nowhere. Nothing's ever happened to him, but people say it's dangerous to walk around alone, without a weapon. There are packs of animals, and they're hungry.

He walks to the lion's den. When he gets there, he sits down on the stone railing. He lights a cigarette and looks out into the empty space.

He thinks of the time his father brought him here. He didn't know what to do with the boy who didn't cry, who hadn't said a thing since his mother died. His sister was a baby, she was looked after by nannies, oblivious to it all.

His father took him to the movies, to the plaza, to the circus, anywhere that was far from home, far from the photos of his smiling mother holding up her architecture diploma, the clothes still on their hangers, the Chagall print she'd picked out to place above the bed. *Paris Through the Window*: there's a cat with a human face, a man flying with a triangular parachute, a colourful window, a dark couple and a man with two faces and a heart in his hand. There's something that speaks to the craziness of the world, a craziness at times cheerful, and cruel, even though all of them are serious. Today, the print hangs in his bedroom.

The zoo was full of families, caramel apples, cotton candy in shades of pink, yellow, blue; laughter, balloons, stuffed kangaroos, whales, bears. His father would say, "Look, Marcos, a tit monkey. Look, Marcos, a coral snake. Look, Marcos, a tiger." He would look without speaking because he felt his father didn't have any words, that the ones he said weren't really there. He intuited without being certain that his father's words were about to break, that they were held together by the thinnest of transparent threads.

When they reached the lion's den, his father stood there watching and didn't say anything. The lionesses were resting in the sun. The lion wasn't there. Someone had a biscuit to feed the animals and tossed it into the den. The lionesses looked on with indifference. They're so far away, he thought, and at that moment, all he wanted was to leap into the den, lie down with the lionesses and go to sleep. He would have liked to pet them. The children shouted, growled, tried to roar, the people piled close together, said "excuse me". But then suddenly everyone went silent. The lion came out of the shadows, out of a cave, and slowly ambled along. He looked at his father and said, "Dad, the lion, the lion's over there, do you see it?" But his father's head was down, he was fading among all those people. And though he wasn't crying, the tears were there, behind the words he couldn't say.

He finishes his cigarette and tosses it into the den. Then he gets up to leave.

Slowly he walks back to his car, his hands in his trouser pockets. He hears a howl. It's in the distance. He stops and looks around to see if he can make anything out.

He arrives at the New Dawn Nursing Home. It's a large house surrounded by well-kept grounds with benches, trees and fountains. He was told that there were once ducks in a small artificial pond. Today the pond is gone. The ducks are too.

When he rings the bell, a nurse answers. He can never remember their names, though they all remember his. "Señor Marcos, how are you doing? Come on in, we'll bring Don Armando over in just a moment."

He made sure that all the employees at the home were nurses. Not caregivers or night attendants with no education or training. That's where he met Cecilia.

The first thing he notices every time he walks in is the faint smell of urine and medication. The artificial odour of the chemicals that keep these bodies breathing. The home is impeccably clean, but he knows the smell of urine is almost impossible to get rid of with the seniors in nappies. He never calls them grandpas.

Not all of them are grandparents, or will be. They're just seniors, people who have been alive for many years, and perhaps that's their only achievement.

The nurse leads him to the waiting room and offers him something to drink. He sits down in an armchair facing a huge window that opens onto a garden. No one goes for a walk in the garden without protection. Some people use umbrellas. The birds aren't violent, but people panic around them. A black bird perches on the branch of a small bush. He hears a gasp. A woman, a senior, a patient at the nursing home is looking fearfully at the bird. It flies off and the senior mumbles something, as though she could protect herself with words. Then she falls asleep in her seat. She appears to have been recently bathed.

He remembers Hitchcock's *The Birds*, and how much of an impact the film had had on him when he saw it, and how he wished it hadn't been prohibited.

He thinks back to when he met Cecilia. He'd been sitting in the same armchair, waiting. Nélida wasn't there and Cecilia was the one who had taken him to his father. In those days his father walked, talked, was somewhat lucid on his visits. When he stood up and saw her, he didn't feel anything in particular. Just another nurse. But then she began to talk and he paid attention. That voice. She talked about the special diet Don Armando was on, about how they were monitoring his blood pressure and giving him regular check-ups, about how he was calmer now. He saw infinite lights surround them and felt that her voice could lift him up. That her voice was a way out of the world.

After what happened with the baby, Cecilia's words became black holes, they began to disappear into themselves.

There's a TV on with no volume. It's a rerun of an old show where the participants have to kill cats with a stick. They risk their lives to win a car. The audience applauds.

He picks up a brochure for the nursing home. It's on a side table, next to the magazines. On the cover, a man and woman are smiling. They're seniors, but not quite elderly. The brochures used to have pictures of seniors frolicking in a meadow, or sitting in a park surrounded by greenery. Today the backdrop is neutral. But the seniors are smiling just like they always did. Inside a circle, in red letters, are the words "Security guaranteed 24/7." It's known that in public nursing homes, when the majority of seniors die, or are left to die, they're sold on the black market. It's the cheapest meat money can buy because it's dry and diseased, full of pharmaceuticals. It's meat with a first and last name. In some cases, a senior's own family members will authorize a private or state-owned nursing home to sell their body and use the proceeds to pay off any debt. There are no longer funerals. It's very difficult to ensure that a body isn't disinterred and eaten. That's why many of the cemeteries were sold and others abandoned. Some still remain as relics of a time when the dead could rest in peace.

He will not allow his father to be cut up.

From the waiting room, he can see the lounge area where the seniors relax. They're sitting and watching television. It's how they spend most of their time. They watch television and wait to die.

There aren't many of them. This was something else he'd made sure of. He didn't want his father in a nursing home full of neglected seniors. But there also aren't many of them because it's the most expensive facility in the city.

Time stifles in this place. The hours and seconds stick to the skin, pierce it. Better to ignore its passing, though that's not possible.

"Hi there, Marcos. How are you doing? It's so nice to see you, dear." Nélida has brought his father over in a wheelchair. She hugs him because she's fond of him, because all the nurses know the story of the man who's not only a dedicated son but who rescued one of the nurses and married her.

After the baby's death, Nélida started hugging him.

He crouches down and looks his father in the eye and takes his hands. "Hi, Dad," he says. His father's gaze is lost, desolate.

"How's Dad, any better?" he says, getting up. "Do you know what prompted it?"

Nélida tells him to take a seat. She leaves his father next to the armchair, looking out the window. They sit close by, at a table with two chairs.

"Don Armando had another episode, dear. Yesterday he took off all his clothes, and when Marta—she's the nurse who works nights—went to look after one of the other residents, your father went to the kitchen and ate the entire birthday cake we'd set aside for a grandpa who's turning ninety."

He covers up his smile. The black bird takes flight and lands on another bush. His father points happily to the bird. He gets up and pushes the wheelchair close to the window. When he sits back down, Nélida looks at him with affection and pity. "Marcos, we're going to have to go back to tying him up at night," she says. He nods. "I need you to sign the authorization form. It's for Don Armando's own good. You know I don't like to do it. But your father is sensitive. He can't go eating whatever he wants, it's not good for him. Besides, today it's a cake, tomorrow it's a knife."

Nélida goes to get the forms.

His father barely speaks now. He emits sounds. Complaints.

The words are there, encapsulated. They're rotting behind the madness.

He sits down in the armchair and looks out the window. Then he takes his father's hand. His father looks at him as though he doesn't know him, but neither does he pull his hand away.

9

He arrives at the processing plant. It's isolated and surrounded by electric fencing. They had it put up because Scavengers kept trying to get in. Before the fence was electrified, the Scavengers would break it, climb over it and cut themselves just to get fresh meat. Now they make do with the leftovers, the pieces that don't have commercial use, with the diseased meat, with what no one would eat, except them.

Before going into the plant, he sits in the car for a few seconds and looks at the complex of buildings. They're white, compact, efficient. There's nothing to indicate that inside them, humans are killed. He remembers the photos of the Salamone Slaughterhouse his mother showed him. The building was destroyed, but the façade remains intact, the word "Slaughterhouse" striking out in silence. Huge and alone, the word resisted, didn't disappear. It held out, refusing to be broken down by the weather, by the wind that perforated the stone, by the climate that ate away at the façade that his mother told him had an art deco influence. The grey letters stand out against the backdrop of the sky. It doesn't matter what the sky looks like, if it's an oppressive blue, or full of clouds, or a rabid black, the word remains, the word that speaks to the implacable truth behind a beautiful building. "Slaughterhouse" because there, slaughter took place. His mother had wanted to renovate the façade of the Cypress Processing Plant, but his father wouldn't agree to it. He felt that a slaughterhouse should go unnoticed and blend in with the landscape, that it should never be called what it really is.

The security guard who works mornings, a man named Oscar, is reading the paper. When Oscar sees him sitting in the car, he closes the paper right away and waves nervously. Oscar opens the door for him and says, in a voice that's a bit forced, "Good morning, Señor Tejo, how are you doing?" He acknowledges the security guard with a movement of the head.

He gets out of the car. Before going in, he has a smoke, his arms propped up on the car roof, still, watching. He wipes the sweat off his forehead.

There's nothing in the vicinity of the processing plant. Nothing that can be seen with the naked eye. There's a space that's been cleared except for a few solitary trees and a rank creek. He's hot, but he smokes slowly, stretching out the minutes before he enters the plant.

He goes straight up to Krieg's office. A few employees greet him on the way. He responds almost without looking at them. He kisses the secretary, Mari, on the cheek. She offers him some coffee and says, "I'll get that for you in just a second, Marcos, I'm really glad to see you. Señor Krieg was starting to get nervous. It happens every time you're on the meat run." He enters the office without knocking and sits down without asking permission. Krieg is on the phone. He smiles and motions that he'll be right with him.

Krieg's words are hard-hitting but scarce. He says little and speaks slowly.

He's one of those people who's not made for life. His face looks like a portrait that turned out all wrong, one the artist crumpled up and tossed into the dustbin. He's someone who doesn't quite fit in anywhere. He's not interested in human contact, which is why he had his office remodelled. First he isolated it, so that only his secretary could hear him and see him. Then he added another door. The door opens to a staircase that takes him straight to the private car park behind the plant. The employees see him infrequently, or not at all.

Working for Krieg, he's seen how the man runs the business to perfection: when it comes to numbers and transactions, he's the best. If it's a question of abstract concepts, market trends, statistics, Krieg excels. He's only interested in edible humans, heads, the product. What he's not interested in is people. He hates saying hello to them, making small talk about the cold or the heat, having to listen to their problems, learn their names, keep track of who's on leave or who's had a child. That's why Krieg needs him. He's the one they all respect and like because none of them knows him, not really. Few of them know he lost a child, that his wife has left, that his father is collapsing into a dark and demented silence.

No one knows he's incapable of killing the female in his barn.

10

Krieg hangs up.

"I have two job applicants waiting. Didn't you see them when you came in?"

"No."

"I want you to give them the test. I'm only interested in hiring the better of the two."

"Got it."

"When that's done give me the updates. This is more pressing."

He gets up to leave but Krieg motions for him to sit down again.

"There's something else. An employee was found with a female."

"Who?"

"One of the night guards."

"There's nothing I can do about it. They're not my responsibility."

"I'm letting you know because I'm going to have to change the security company again."

"How did they catch him?"

"The security footage. We've started checking it every morning."

"And the female?"

"He raped her to death. Then he tossed her in one of

the group cages with the others. He didn't even put her in the right cage, the idiot."

"What happens now?"

"The FSA has to be called and a police report filed for destruction of moveable property."

"The security company will have to reimburse us for the value of the female."

"Right, that too, especially because she was an FGP."

When he gets up to leave, he sees Mari with the coffee. She comes across as fragile, but he knows that if this woman were told to slaughter the whole shipment, she'd do it on her own, without a single muscle in her body trembling. He motions to her to forget the coffee and asks to be introduced to the job applicants. "They're in the waiting room, didn't you see them when you came in?" she asks, and offers to take him down. He says he'll go alone.

Two young men are waiting silently. He introduces himself and tells them to follow him. He says that they're going to take a short tour of the processing plant. As they walk to the unloading yard, he asks them why they want the job. He doesn't expect elaborate answers. He knows that applicants are in short supply, there's constant turnover, few people can handle working in a place like this. They're driven by the need to earn money; they know the job pays well. But before long, necessity isn't enough. They'd rather earn less and do something that doesn't involve cleaning human entrails.

The taller of the two applicants says he needs the money because his girlfriend is pregnant and he has to start saving.

The other man looks on with a heavy silence. He doesn't answer right away and then says that a friend who works at a hamburger factory suggested he apply. He doesn't believe the man, not for a second.

They reach the unloading yard. Men are using shovels to pick up excrement from the last shipment. They place it in bags. Other men are washing the cage trailers and the floor with hoses. All of them are dressed in white and wearing black rubber boots up to their knees. The men greet him. He nods without smiling. The taller applicant goes to cover his nose, but right away he lowers his hand and asks why they keep the excrement. The other man looks on silently.

"It's for manure," he tells the applicant and then explains that this is where the shipment is unloaded, weighed and branded. The heads are also shaved because their hair is sold. Then they're brought to the resting cages where they take it easy for a day. "The meat from a stressed head is tough or tastes bad, it becomes low-grade meat," he tells them. "It's at this point that the ante-mortem inspection is done."

"Ante what?" the taller applicant asks.

He explains that any product that shows signs of disease needs to be removed. The applicants nod. "We separate them into special cages. If they get better, they return to the slaughter cycle, and if they don't, they're discarded."

"By 'they're discarded', do you mean they're slaughtered?" the taller man asks.

"Yes."

"Why aren't they returned to the breeding centre?"

"Because transport is expensive. The breeding centre is notified of the heads that had to be thrown out and later they're discounted."

"Why aren't they treated?"

"Because it's too large an investment."

"Do the heads ever arrive dead?" the taller applicant continues.

He looks at the man somewhat surprised. The job applicants don't usually ask questions like these and the fact that this one is doing so intrigues him. "Few arrive dead, but every so often we get one. When that happens, the FSA is informed and they come take the head away." He knows that this is the official truth, which makes it a relative truth. He knows (because he sees to it) that the employees leave a few heads for the Scavengers, who slaughter the meat with machetes and take what they can. They don't care that the meat is diseased; they run the risk because they can't afford to buy it. He lets it go and tries to see the gesture as an act of charity or perhaps of mercy. But he also does it as a means of appeasing the Scavengers and their hunger. The craving for meat is dangerous.

As they walk to the resting cage sector, he tells them that at first they'll have to do simple jobs, related to cleaning and rubbish collection. Once they've demonstrated their ability and loyalty, they'll be taught other tasks.

There's a sharp, penetrating smell to the resting cage sector. He thinks it's the smell of fear. They climb a set of stairs to a suspended balcony from where it's possible to observe the shipment. He asks them not to talk loudly because the heads need to be kept calm. Sudden sounds disturb them and when they're edgy, they're more difficult to handle. The cages are below them. The heads are still agitated after the journey, despite the fact that unloading took place in the early hours of the morning. They move about in a frightened way.

He explains that when the heads arrive, they're given a spray wash and then examined. They need to fast, he adds, and are given a liquid diet to reduce intestinal content and lower the risk of contamination when they're handled after slaughter. He tries to count the number of times he's repeated this sentence in his life.

The shorter applicant points to heads that have been branded with a green cross. "What do the green marks on their chests mean?"

"Those heads have been selected for the game reserve. The specialists examine them and pick the ones in the best physical condition. The hunters need prey that challenges them, they want to chase after the heads, they're not interested in sitting targets."

"So that's why most of them are males," the taller man says.

"That's right, females are generally submissive. They've tried with impregnated females and the result is very different because they become vicious. Every so often we get requests for them."

"And what about the ones with the black crosses?" the shorter man asks.

"They're for the laboratory."

The man tries to ask him something else, but he keeps walking. He has no intention of saying anything about that place, about the Valka Laboratory. Even if he wanted to, he wouldn't be able to do it.

The employees examining the shipment greet him from the cages. "Tomorrow the heads that have just arrived will be taken to the blue cages and from there they'll go directly to the slaughter," he tells the applicants, as they go downstairs and walk to the box room.

The smaller man slows his step to look at the heads in the blue cages and motions to him to come over. The man wants to know if the heads are going to be slaughtered that day. "Yes," he says, and the man looks at them silently.

On the way to the box sector, they pass special cages that are red in colour. The cages are large and each of them contains a single head. Before the applicants can ask, he tells them that this is export-quality meat, that these heads are First Generation Pure. "It's the most expensive meat on the market because it takes many years to raise the heads," he says. Then he has to explain that all the other meat is genetically modified, so that the product grows faster and there's a profit.

"But then is the meat we eat completely artificial? Is it synthetic meat?" the taller applicant asks.

"Well, no. I wouldn't say it's artificial or synthetic. I'd say modified. It doesn't taste all that different from FGP meat, though FGP is upper grade, for refined palates." The two men stand there in silence, looking at the cages containing heads that have the letters FGP written all over their bodies. One set of initials per year of growth.

He notices the taller applicant looking a little pale. It's not likely he'll be able to handle what comes next, he thinks, he'll probably vomit, or faint. He asks the man if he's okay.

"Yeah, I'm fine. I'm fine," the man answers.

The same thing happens every time with the weaker applicant. The men need the money, but the money is not enough.

He's so tired it could kill him, but he keeps walking.

11

They enter the box sector, but stop in the lounge, which has a large window that faces the desensitization room. The place is so white it blinds them.

He has them wait there and the shorter man asks why they can't go in. The taller man takes a seat. He answers that only authorized staff wearing the required uniform can go in, that all the necessary measures are taken to ensure the meat isn't contaminated.

Sergio, one of the stunners, waves to him and then comes into the lounge. He's dressed in white, and has on black boots, a face mask, plastic apron, helmet and gloves. Sergio gives him a hug. "Tejo, where have you been, mate?"

"On the meat run, dealing with clients and suppliers. Let me introduce you."

He goes for the occasional beer with Sergio. He thinks he's a genuine guy, one who doesn't smirk at him for being the boss's right-hand man, who's not trying to get something from him, who has no problem telling him what he thinks. When the baby died, Sergio didn't look at him with pity, or say, "Leo is a little angel now." He wasn't silent around him, not knowing what to do, and he didn't avoid him, or treat him any differently. Sergio hugged him and took him to a bar and got him drunk and didn't stop telling him jokes until the two of them laughed so hard they cried. The pain was still there, but he knew that in Sergio he had a friend. Once he asked him why he worked as a stunner. Sergio answered that it was either the heads or his family. It was the only thing he knew how to do and it paid well. Whenever he felt remorse he thought of his children and how the work enabled him to give them a better life. He said that even though the original meat, from before the product was bred, didn't eliminate overpopulation, poverty and hunger, it did help fight them. He said that everything has a purpose in this life and the purpose of meat is to be slaughtered and then eaten. He said that thanks to his work, people were fed and that was something he was proud of. Sergio kept talking, but he couldn't listen any longer.

They went out to celebrate when Sergio's eldest daughter started university. He asked himself, while they raised their glasses in a toast, how many heads had paid for the education of Sergio's children, how many times he'd had to swing a club in his life. He offered Sergio the chance to work by his side, as his assistant, but the man was blunt: "I prefer striking." He valued the answer and didn't ask for an explanation because Sergio's words are simple, clear. They're words that don't have sharp edges.

Sergio goes up to the applicants and shakes their hands. "His job is one of the most important, stunning the heads. He strikes them unconscious so their throats can be slit. Go ahead and show them, Sergio," he says and tells the men to climb up steps that have been built below the window. This way they'll be able to see what happens inside the box.

Sergio enters the box room and gets up onto the platform. He grabs the club. Then he shouts, "Send in the next one!" A guillotine door opens and a naked female, barely twenty years of age, walks in. She's wet and her hands are held behind her back with a cable tie. She's been shaved. Inside the box there's very little space. It's almost impossible for her to move. Sergio places the stainless steel shackle, which runs along a vertical rail, around the female's neck and clamps it shut. The female trembles, shakes a little, tries to free herself. She opens her mouth.

Sergio looks her in the eye and pats her a few times on the head, almost like he's petting her. He says something to her they can't hear, or sings to her. The female becomes still, she calms down. Sergio raises the club and hits her on the forehead. It's a sharp strike. So swift and silent it's crazy. The female is knocked unconscious. Her body goes slack and when Sergio opens the shackle, it falls to the ground. The automatic door opens outwards and the base of the box tilts to expel the body, which slides onto the floor.

An employee enters and binds her feet with straps that are attached to chains. He cuts the cable tie holding her hands together and presses a button. The body is raised and transported face down to another room via a system of rails. The employee looks up into the lounge and waves at him. He doesn't remember the man's name, but knows he hired him a few months back.

The employee gets a hose and rinses off the box and floor, which have been splattered with excrement.

The taller applicant climbs down from the steps and takes a seat on a chair, his head hanging. Now is when this man vomits, he thinks, but the man gets up, composes himself. Sergio comes in with a smile, proud of the demonstration. "So what did you think? Who wants to give it a try?" he says.

The shorter man steps forward and says, "I do."

Sergio laughs loudly and says, "Not so fast, mate, it'll be a while before you're doing that." The man looks disappointed. "Let me explain a few things to you. If you strike them dead, you've gone and ruined the meat. And if you don't knock them unconscious and they're alive when they go to the slaughter, you've also ruined the meat. Got that?" He gives the man a hug and shakes him a little, laughing. "Kids today, Tejo. They want to take on the world and don't even know how to walk." All of them laugh, except for the shorter applicant. Sergio explains that beginners use a captive bolt pistol. "There's a smaller margin of error, but the meat doesn't turn out quite as tender. That make sense? Ricardo, he's the stunner who's taking a rest outside at the moment, uses the pistol and is training to use the club. He's been here for six months." Sergio finishes off by saying, "The club is only for those who know what they're doing."

The taller man asks Sergio what he said to the meat, why he spoke to it. "Meat," he thinks with surprise, while they wait for Sergio's answer, and wonders why the man called the stunned female that, and not a head, or a product. Then Sergio says that every stunner has his secret when it comes to calming down the heads. He says that every new stunner has to find his method.

"Why don't they scream?" the man asks.

He doesn't want to answer, he wants to be somewhere else, but he's there. Sergio is the one who says something: "They don't have vocal cords."

The shorter applicant climbs up the steps and looks into the box room again. He puts his hands up against the window. There's eagerness in his gaze. There's impatience in it.

He thinks this man is dangerous. Someone who wants to assassinate that badly is someone who's unstable, who won't take to the routine of killing, to the automatic and dispassionate act of slaughtering humans.

12

They leave the lounge. He tells them that they're moving on to the slaughter sector. "Are we going in?" the shorter man asks.

He looks at the man severely. "No," he says, "we're not going in, because as I told you, our attire doesn't meet regulations."

The man looks at the floor and doesn't answer, then impatiently puts his hands in his trouser pockets. He suspects this man is a fake applicant. Every so often people pretend to want the job so they can witness the killing. People who enjoy the process, for whom it's a source of curiosity, an interesting anecdote to add to their lives. He thinks they're people who don't have the courage to accept and take on the weight of the work.

They walk through a hallway with a wide window that looks directly into the slitting room. The workers are dressed in white, inside the white room. But the apparent cleanliness is stained with the tonnes of blood that fall into the bleeding trough and splatter the walls, the coveralls, the floor, the hands.

The heads enter via an automatic rail. Three bodies are hanging face down. The first has had its throat slit, the other two wait their turn. One of these is the female Sergio has just stunned. The worker presses a button and the body that's been bled dry follows its course along the rail while the next body moves into place above the trough. With a swift movement, the worker slits the head's throat. The body trembles slightly. The blood falls into the trough. It stains the worker's apron, trousers and boots.

The shorter man asks what they do with the blood. He decides to ignore the man. The taller applicant answers for him, and says, "They use it to make fertilizer." He looks at this man, who smiles and explains that his father worked briefly at a processing plant, one of the old ones, and that he taught him a thing or two. When he says "one of the old ones", he lowers his head and his voice, as though he feels sadness or resignation.

"Cow blood was used to make fertilizer," he tells the man. "This blood has other uses." He doesn't say what they are.

"Like to make some good blood sausage, am I right?" the shorter applicant says. He glares at the man and doesn't answer.

He looks into the slitting room and sees the worker talking distractedly to another employee. It's taking too long, he realizes. The female that Sergio stunned begins to move. The worker doesn't see this. She shakes, slowly at first, and then more forcefully. The movement is so violent that she frees her feet from the loose straps that hold her up. She falls with a thud. She trembles on the floor and her white skin gets smeared with the blood of those whose throats were slit before her. The female raises an arm. She tries to stand up. The worker turns around and looks at her with indifference. He grabs a captive bolt pistol, puts it to her forehead and pulls the trigger. Then he hangs her back up.

The shorter applicant goes up to the window and watches the scene with a smirk on his face. The taller man covers his mouth.

While the applicants are standing there, he knocks on the glass. The worker jumps. He hadn't seen his boss in the window and knows the mistake could cost him his job. He motions to the worker to come out. The man asks for a replacement and leaves the slitting room.

He addresses the worker by name and tells him that what just happened can't happen again. "This meat died in fear and it's going to taste bad. You ruined Sergio's work by taking too long." The worker looks at the floor and tells him that it was a mistake, apologizes, says it won't happen again. He tells the man that until further notice he'll be moved to the offal room. The worker can't hide the look of disgust on his face, but he nods.

The female that Sergio stunned is now being bled dry. There's still one head whose throat needs to be slit.

He sees the taller man crouch down and put his head between his hands. The man remains there, and he goes over and pats him on the back, asks if he's okay. The man doesn't answer and only signals that he needs a minute. The other applicant continues to watch, fascinated, unaware of what's happening behind him. The taller man stands up. He's gone white and beads of sweat have formed on his forehead. But he's recovered and goes back to watching.

They see the way the female's bloodless body moves along the rail until a worker undoes the straps around her feet and the body falls into a scalding tank where other corpses are floating in boiling water. A different employee plunges the corpses below the surface with a stick and moves them around. The taller applicant asks if their lungs fill with contaminated water when they're pushed below the surface.

"Smart guy," he thinks, and tells the man that yes, water does get in, but only a little, because they're no longer breathing. He says that the plant's next investment will be a spray-scalding system. "With these systems scalding occurs individually and vertically," he explains.

The worker places one of the floating bodies inside the grill of the loading container, which lifts up and tosses it into the dehairing machine, where it begins to spin while a system of rollers equipped with scraper paddles removes the hair. This part of the process still gets to him. The bodies are spun at high speeds; it's almost as if they were performing a strange and cryptic dance.

13

He motions to the applicants to follow him. The next stop is the offal room. They walk there very slowly and he tells them that the product is used almost in its entirety. "Hardly anything goes to waste," he says. The shorter applicant stops to watch a worker use a blowtorch on the scalded corpses. Once they're entirely hairless, they can be gutted.

On the way there they walk through the cutting room. The rooms are all connected by a rail that moves the bodies from one stage to the next. Through the wide windows, they see the way the head and extremities of the female stunned by Sergio are cut off with a saw.

They stop to watch.

A worker picks up her head and takes it to another table where he removes her eyes and puts them on a tray with a label that says "Eyes". He opens her mouth, cuts out her tongue and places it on a tray with a label that says "Tongues". He cuts off her ears and sets them down on a tray with a label that says "Ears". The worker picks up an awl and a hammer and carefully taps the bottom of her head. He continues in this manner until he has cracked a portion of her skull, and then he carefully removes her brain and leaves it on a tray with a label that says "Brains".

Her head is now empty and he places it on ice in a drawer that says "Heads".

“What do you do with the heads?” the shorter applicant asks, barely containing his excitement.

He answers automatically: “A number of things. One is sending them to the provinces where they still cook heads like they used to, in pits in the ground.”

The taller applicant says, “I’ve never had heads cooked that way but I hear it’s pretty good. There’s only a little meat, but it’s cheap and tasty if done well.”

Another worker has already gathered and cleaned the female’s hands and feet, and placed them in drawers with their respective labels. Arms and legs are sold to butchers attached to the carcasses. He explains that all of the products are washed and checked by inspectors before they’re refrigerated. He points to a man who’s dressed like the rest of the workers but is carrying a folder in which he jots down information, and a certification stamp that every so often he takes out and uses.

The female that Sergio stunned has now been flayed and is unrecognizable. Without skin and extremities, she’s becoming a carcass. They see the way a worker picks up the skin that was removed by a machine and carefully stretches it in the large drawers.

They continue walking. The wide windows now face either the intermediary room or the cutting room. The flayed bodies move along the rails. The workers make a precise cut from the pubis to the solar plexus. The taller applicant asks him why there are two workers per body. He explains that one worker makes the cut and the other stitches the anus shut to prevent expulsions from contaminating the product. The other applicant laughs and says, “I wouldn’t want that job.”

He thinks that he wouldn't even hire the man for that job. The taller applicant has had enough as well and looks at him with contempt.

The intestines, stomachs, pancreases fall onto a stainless steel table and are taken to the offal room by employees.

The bodies that have been cut open move along the rails. On another table, a worker slices the upper cavity. He takes out the kidneys and liver, separates the ribs, cuts out the heart, oesophagus and lungs.

They continue walking. When they reach the offal room, they see stainless steel tables. Tubes are connected to the tables and water flows over the surface of them. White entrails have been placed on top of them. The workers slide the entrails around in the water. It looks like a sea that's slowly boiling, that moves at its own rhythm. The entrails are inspected, cleaned, flushed, pulled apart, graded, cut, measured and stored. The three of them watch the workers pick up the intestines and cover them in layers of salt before storing them in drawers. They watch the workers scrape away the mesenteric fat. They watch them inject compressed air into the intestines to make sure they haven't been punctured. They watch them wash the stomachs and cut them open to release an amorphous substance, greenish-brown in colour, that's then discarded. They watch them clean the empty, broken stomachs, which are then dried, reduced, cut into strips and compressed to make something like an edible sponge.

In another, smaller room, they see red entrails hanging from hooks. The workers inspect them, wash them, certify them, store them.

He always asks himself what it would be like to spend most of the day storing human hearts in a box. What do the workers think about? Are they aware that what they hold in their hands was beating just moments ago? Do they care? Then he thinks that he actually spends most of his life supervising a group of people who, following his orders, slit the throats, gut and cut up women and men as if doing so were completely natural. One can get used to almost anything, except the death of a child.

How many heads do they have to kill each month so he can pay for his father's nursing home? How many humans do they have to slaughter for him to forget how he laid Leo down in his cot, tucked him in, sang him a lullaby, and the next day saw he had died in his sleep? How many hearts need to be stored in boxes for the pain to be transformed into something else? But the pain, he intuits, is the only thing that keeps him breathing.

Without the sadness, he has nothing left.

14

He tells the two men that they're nearing the end of the slaughter process. Next they'll stop by the room where the carcasses are divided into parts. Through a small square window they can see into a room that's narrower, but just as white and well-lit as the others. Two men with chainsaws cut the bodies in half. The men are dressed in regulation attire, but with helmets and black plastic boots. Plastic visors cover their faces. They appear to be concentrating. Other employees inspect and store the spinal columns that were removed before the cut was made.

One of the saw operators looks at him but doesn't acknowledge his presence. The man's name is Pedro Manzanillo. He picks up the chainsaw and slices the body more forcefully, as if with rage, though the cut he makes is precise. Manzanillo is always on edge when he's around. He knows this and tries not to cross paths with the man, though it's unavoidable.

He tells the applicants that after the carcasses have been cut in half, they're washed, inspected, sealed, weighed and placed in the cooling chamber to ensure they're kept cold enough. "But doesn't the cold make the meat tough?" the shorter applicant asks.

He explains the chemical processes that allow the meat to remain tender as a result of the cold. He uses words like lactic acid, myosin, ATP, glycogen, enzymes. The man nods like he understands. “Our job is done when the different parts of the product are transported to their respective destinations,” he says, so he can end the tour and go for a cigarette.

Manzanillo puts the chainsaw down on a table and looks at him again. He holds the man’s gaze because he knows he did what needed to be done and he doesn’t feel guilty about it. Manzanillo used to work with another saw operator who everyone called “Ency” because he was like an encyclopedia. He knew the meanings of complex words and on break was always reading a book. At first the others laughed at him, but then he began to describe the plot of whatever he was reading and he captivated them. Ency and Manzanillo were like brothers. They lived in the same neighbourhood, their wives and kids were friends. They drove to work together and made a good team. But Ency began to change. Little by little. As the man’s boss, he was the only one who noticed at first. Ency seemed quieter. When he was on break, he’d stare at the shipment in the resting cages. He lost weight. There were bags under his eyes. He started to pause before cutting the carcasses. He’d get sick and miss work. Ency needed to be confronted and one day he took the man aside and asked him what was going on. Ency said it was nothing. The next day everything seemed to be back to normal and for a while he thought the man was fine. But then one afternoon Ency said he was going on break and took the chainsaw without anyone noticing. He went to the resting cages and began to cut them open. Whenever a worker tried to stop him, he threatened them with the chainsaw. A few heads escaped, but the majority stayed in their cages. They were confused and frightened. Ency was shouting, "You're not animals. They're going to kill you. Run. You need to escape," as if the heads could understand what he was saying. Someone was able to hit him over the head with a club and he was knocked unconscious. His subversive act only succeeded in delaying the slaughter by a few hours. The only ones to benefit were the employees, who got to take a break from their work and enjoy the interruption. The heads that escaped didn't get very far and were put back in their cages.

He had to fire Ency because someone who's been broken can't be fixed. He did speak to Krieg and make sure he arranged and paid for psychological care. But within a month, Ency had shot himself. His wife and kids had to leave the neighbourhood, and since then Manzanillo has looked at him with genuine hatred. He respects Manzanillo for it. He thinks it'll be cause for concern when the man stops looking at him this way, when the hatred doesn't keep him going any longer. Because hatred gives one strength to go on; it maintains the fragile structure, it weaves the threads together so that emptiness doesn't take over everything. He wishes he could hate someone for the death of his son. But who can he blame for a sudden death? He tried to hate God but he doesn't believe in God. He tried to hate all of humanity for being so fragile and ephemeral but he couldn't keep it up because hating everyone is the same as hating no one. He also wishes he could break like Ency, but his collapse never comes.

The shorter applicant is quiet, his face is pressed up against the window and he's watching the bodies being cut in two. There's a smile on his face that he no longer bothers to hide. He wishes he could feel what this man does. He wishes he could feel happiness, or excitement, when he promotes a worker who used to wash blood off the floor to a position of sorting and storing organs in boxes. Or he wishes he could at least be indifferent to it all. He looks at the applicant more closely and sees he's hiding a phone under his jacket. How could this have happened if security pats them down, asks for their phones and tells them they can't film anything or take pictures? He goes up to the man and grabs hold of the phone. He throws it to the ground and breaks it. Then he grabs him forcefully by the arm and, containing his fury, says into his ear, "Don't come here again. I'm going to send your contact info and photo to all the processing plants I know." The man turns around to face him and at no point does he show surprise, or embarrassment, or say a word. He looks at him brazenly and smiles.

15

He takes the applicants to the exit. But first he calls the head of security and tells him to come get the shorter man. He explains what happened and the security guard tells him not to worry, he'll take care of it. They'll need to have a talk, he tells the guard, since this shouldn't have happened. He makes a mental note to discuss it with Krieg. Outsourcing security personnel is a mistake, he's already told Krieg this. He'll have to tell him again.

The shorter applicant is no longer smiling, but neither does he put up a fight when he's taken away.

He says goodbye to the taller man with a handshake, adding, "You'll be hearing from us." The man thanks him without much conviction. It's always this way, he thinks, but any other response would be abnormal.

No one who's in their right mind would be happy to do this job.

16

He steps outside for a cigarette before going up to give Krieg the reports. His phone rings. It's his mother-in-law. He answers the call and says, "Hi, Graciela," without looking at the screen. On the other end there's silence, at once serious and intense. That's when he realizes it's Cecilia.

"Hi, Marcos."

It's the first time she's called since she went to stay with her mother. She looks haggard.

"Hi." He knows it's going to be a difficult conversation and takes another drag on his cigarette.

"How are you?"

"I'm here at the plant. What about you?"

There's a pause before she answers. A long pause. "I see you're there," she says, though she's not looking at the screen. For a few seconds, she's quiet. Then she speaks, but she doesn't look him in the eye. "I'm not well," she says, "still not well. I don't think I'm ready to come back."

"Why don't you let me come visit?"

"I need to be alone."

"I miss you."

The words are a black hole, a hole that absorbs every sound, every particle, every breath. She doesn't answer.

He says, "It happened to me too. I lost him too."

She cries silently. She covers the screen with one hand, and he hears her whisper, "I can't take any more." A pit opens up and he's free-falling, everywhere there are sharp edges. She gives the phone to her mother.

"Hi, Marcos. She's having a really tough time, forgive her."

"It's okay, Graciela."

"Take care, Marcos. She'll get there."

They hang up.

He stays where he is for a little while longer. The employees walk by and look at him, but he doesn't care. He's in one of the rest areas, outdoors, where you can smoke. He watches the treetops move in the wind that alleviates the heat a little. He likes the rhythm, the sound of the leaves brushing against each other. There are only a few trees—four surrounded by nothing—but they're right next to each other.

He knows Cecilia will never get better. He knows she's broken, that the pieces of her have no way of mending.

The first thing he thinks of is the medicine they'd kept in the fridge. How they'd brought it home in a special container, taking care not to break the cold chain, hopeful, deeply in debt. He thinks of the first time she asked him to give her an injection in the stomach. She'd given millions of them, trillions, countless injections, but she'd wanted him to inaugurate the ritual, the start of it all. His hand had trembled a little because he hadn't wanted it to hurt, but she'd said, "Go on, dear, just put the needle in, go on, you've got this, it's no big deal." She'd grabbed a fold in her stomach and he'd put the needle in and it had hurt, the medicine was cold and she'd felt it enter her body, but she'd hidden it with a smile because it was the beginning of possibility, of the future.

Cecilia's words were like a river of lights, an aerial torrent, like fireflies glowing. She'd tell him, when they didn't yet know they'd have to turn to the treatments, that she wanted their children to have his eyes but her nose, his mouth but her hair. He'd laugh because she'd laugh, and with their laughter, his father and the nursing home, the processing plant and the heads, the blood and the stunners' sharp strikes would disappear.

The other image that comes to him like an explosion is Cecilia's face when she opened the envelope and saw the results of the Anti-Mullerian hormone test. She didn't understand how the number could be so low. She looked at the piece of paper, unable to speak, until very slowly, she said, "I'm young, I should be producing more eggs." But she was disconcerted, because as a nurse she knew that youth doesn't guarantee anything. She looked at him, her eyes asking for help, and he took the piece of paper from her, folded it, put it on the table and told her not to worry, that everything was going to be okay. She started to cry and he just held her and kissed her on the forehead and the face, and said, "Everything's going to be okay," even though he knew it wouldn't be.

After that came more injections, pills, low-quality eggs, toilets and screens with naked women on them, and the pressure to fill the plastic cup, baptisms they didn't attend, the question, "So when's the first child coming along?" repeated ad nauseum, operating rooms he wasn't allowed to enter so that he could hold her hand and she wouldn't feel so alone, more debt, other people's babies, the babies of those who could, fluid retention, mood swings, conversations about the possibility of adopting, phone calls to the bank, children's birthday parties they wanted to escape, more hormones, chronic fatigue and more unfertilized eggs, tears, hurtful words, Mothers' Days in silence, the hope for an embryo, the list of possible names, Leonardo if it was a boy, Aria if it was a girl, pregnancy tests thrown helplessly into the bin, fights, the search for an egg donor, questions about genetic identity, letters from the bank, the waiting, the fears, the acceptance that maternity isn't a question of chromosomes, the mortgage, the pregnancy, the birth, the euphoria, the happiness, the death.

17

He gets home late.

When he opens the door to the barn, he sees the female curled up, sleeping. He changes her water and replaces her food. She wakes with a start at the sound of the balanced feed hitting the metal bowl. She doesn't move closer and looks at him in fear.

She needs to be washed, he thinks, but not now, not today. Today he has something more important to do.

He leaves the door of the barn open on his way out. The female follows him slowly. The rope stops her at the entrance.

Back in the house, he goes straight to his son's room. He picks up the cot and takes it out to the yard. Then he gets the axe and kerosene from the barn. The female is on her feet, watching him.

He stands next to the cot, paralysed in the middle of the star-filled night. The lights in the sky in all their appalling beauty crush him. He goes into the house and opens a bottle of whisky.

Now he's next to the cot again. There are no tears. He looks at it and takes a sip from the bottle. He starts with the axe, feels a need to destroy the cot. As he breaks it into pieces, he thinks of Leo's tiny feet in his hands right after he was born.

After that he douses the cot in kerosene and lights a

match. He takes another sip. The sky is like an ocean that's gone still.

He watches the hand-painted drawings disappear. The hugging bear and duck burn, lose their shape, evaporate.

The female is watching him. He sees her there. She seems fascinated by the fire. He goes into the barn and she curls up in fright. He remains on his feet, swaying. The female trembles. And if he destroys her too? She's his, he can do whatever he wants. He can kill her, slaughter her, make her suffer. He picks up the axe. Looks at her silently. This female is a problem. He raises the axe. Then he moves closer and cuts the rope.

He goes out and lies down in the grass beneath the silence of the lights in the sky, millions of them, frozen, dead. The sky is made of glass, glass that's opaque and solid. The moon seems a strange god.

He no longer cares if the female escapes. He no longer cares if Cecilia comes back.

The last thing he sees is the door to the barn and the female, that woman, looking at him. It seems like she's crying. But there's no way she understands what's happening, she doesn't know what a cot is. She doesn't know anything.

When only the embers remain, he's asleep in the grass.

18

He opens his eyes, then closes them again. The light hurts. His head is pounding. He's hot. There's a stabbing pain in his right temple. He lies still, trying to remember why he's outside. Then a hazy image appears in his mind. A stone in his chest. That's the image. It's the dream he had. He sits up with his eyes still closed. He tries to open them, but can't. For a few seconds, he's still, his head resting on his knees, his arms wrapped around them. His mind is blank until he remembers the dream with terrifying clarity.

He's naked and walks into an empty room. The walls are stained with humidity and something brown that could be blood. The floor is dirty and broken. His father is in the corner, sitting on a wooden bench. He's naked and is looking at the floor. He tries to go to his father, but can't move. He tries to call him, but can't speak. In another corner, a wolf is eating some meat. Whenever he looks at the wolf, the animal raises its head and snarls. It bares its fangs. The wolf is eating something that's moving, that's alive. He looks closer. It's his son, who's crying but not making a sound. He grows desperate. He wants to save the infant but is immobile, mute. He tries to shout. His father gets up and walks in circles around the room, without looking at him, without looking at his grandson, who's being torn to pieces by the wolf. He cries, but no tears fall, he shouts, wants to climb out of his body, but can't. A man appears with a saw.

The man could be Manzanillo, but he can't see his face. It's blurred. There's a light, a sun hanging from the roof. The sun moves, creating an ellipse of yellow light. He stops thinking about his son, it's as though he never existed. The man who could be Manzanillo cuts his chest open. He feels nothing. Just checks to make sure the job was done well. He gives Manzanillo a congratulatory handshake. Sergio comes in and looks at him closely. He appears to be deep in concentration. Without saying anything to him, Sergio bends down and reaches into his chest. He examines it, moves his fingers, pokes around. Sergio yanks out his heart. He eats a piece. The blood spurts from Sergio's mouth. His heart is still beating, but Sergio throws it to the ground. While he squashes it, Sergio speaks into his ear, and says, "There's nothing worse than not being able to see yourself." Cecilia comes into the room with a black stone. Her face is Spanel's, but he knows it's her. She smiles. The sun moves more quickly. The ellipse gets bigger. The stone shines. It beats. The wolf howls. His father sits down and looks at the floor. Cecilia opens his chest up even more and puts the stone inside it. She's beautiful, he's never seen her so radiant. She turns around, he doesn't want her to leave. He tries to call her, but can't. Cecilia looks at him happily, picks up a club and stuns him right in the middle of the forehead. He falls, but the floor opens up and he keeps falling because the stone in his chest plunges him into a white abyss.

He raises his head and opens his eyes. Then he closes them again. He never remembers his dreams, not with such clarity. He puts his hands behind his neck. It was just a dream, he thinks, but a feeling of instability moves through him. An archaic fear.

He looks to one side and sees the ashes of the cot. He looks to the other side and sees the female lying very close to his body. He gets up with a start, but he's not steady on his feet and sits back down. The thoughts come quickly: What did I do? Why is she loose? Why didn't she escape? What is she doing next to me?

The female is curled up in sleep. She looks peaceful. Her white skin glistens in the sun. He goes to touch her, he wants to touch her, but she trembles slightly, as though she were dreaming, and he moves his hand away. He looks at her forehead, where she's been branded. It's the symbol of property, of value.

He looks at her straight hair, which hasn't yet been cut and sold. It's long, and filthy.

There's a certain purity to this being who's unable to speak, he thinks, as his finger traces the outline of her shoulder, arm, hips, legs, until it reaches her feet. He doesn't touch her. His finger hovers a centimetre above her skin, a centimetre above the initials, the FGPs scattered all over her body. She's gorgeous, he thinks, but her beauty is useless. She won't taste any better because she's beautiful. The thought doesn't surprise him, he doesn't even linger on it. It's what he thinks whenever there's a head he notices at the processing plant. The odd female that stands out among the many that move through the place every day.

He lies down very close to her, but doesn't touch her. He feels the heat of her body, her slow and unhurried breath. He moves a little closer and begins to breathe with her rhythm. Slowly, slower still. He can smell her. She has a strong smell because she's dirty, but he likes it, thinks of the intoxicating scent of jasmine, wild and sharp, vibrant. His breath quickens. Something about this excites him, this closeness, this possibility.

He gets up suddenly. The female wakes with a start and looks at him in confusion. He grabs her arm and takes her to the barn, not with violence, but decisively. Then he closes the door and walks to the house. He showers quickly, brushes his teeth, dresses, takes two aspirin and gets into the car.

It's his day off, but he drives to the city, without thinking, without stopping.

When he arrives at Spanel Butchers, it's still very early and the shop isn't open. But he knows she sleeps there. He rings the bell and El Perro opens the door. He pushes the assistant aside without saying hello and goes straight to the room at the back. He closes the door. Locks it.

Spanel is standing next to the wooden table. She's clearly relaxed, as though she's been expecting him. There's a knife in her hand and she's cutting an arm that hangs from a hook. It looks very fresh, as though she yanked it off a few seconds prior. The arm isn't from a processing plant because it hasn't been bled dry or flayed. There's blood on the table, and on the floor. The drops fall slowly. A puddle is forming and the only sound in the room is the blood from the table splattering onto the floor.

He moves towards Spanel, as though he's going to say something, but he puts his hand through her hair and grabs her by the nape of her neck. He uses force to hold her there, and he kisses her. It's a ravenous kiss, at first, full of rage. She tries to resist, but only a little. He pulls off her bloodstained apron and kisses her again. He kisses her like he wants to break her, but he moves slowly. He undoes her shirt while he bites her neck. She arches her back, trembles, but doesn't make a sound. He turns her to face the table and pushes her onto it. Then he lowers her trousers and slides her underwear down. She's breathing heavily, waiting, but he decides to make her suffer, that he wants to enter her behind the cold of her cutting words. Spanel looks at him, imploring him, almost begging him, but he ignores her. He walks to the other end of the table, grabs her by the hair and forces her to unzip him with her mouth. The blood dripping from the arm falls right past the edge of the table, between her lips and his crotch. He takes off his boots, his jeans, and then his shirt. Naked, he steps towards the table. The blood drips onto him, stains him. He shows her where to clean, there, where the flesh is hard. She obeys and licks him. Carefully at first, then desperately, as though the blood that stains everything weren't enough and she needed more. He grabs her hair with more force and motions for her to slow down. She obeys.

What he wants is for her to scream, for her skin to cease being a still and empty sea, for her words to crack open, dissolve.

He goes back to the other end of the table. He removes her trousers, rips off her underwear and opens her legs. Then he hears a sound and sees El Perro looking in through the window in the door. Good for him, he thinks, carrying out his role of faithful animal, of docile servant protecting his owner. He takes pleasure in El Perro's blind stare, in the possibility of the man attacking once and for all.

Then he thrusts. Just once, precisely. She keeps quiet, trembles, contains herself. The blood continues to drip down from the table.

El Perro tries to open the door. It's locked. The man's rage is visible, palpable. There are fangs in El Perro's eyes, he can see them, and relishes the man's desperation. He continues to glare at El Perro and yanks Spanel's hair. She claws silently at the table, gets blood under her nails.

He turns Spanel around and takes a few steps back. Then he looks at her. He sits down on a chair and she moves towards him, stops right above his legs. Then suddenly, he's on his feet, the chair knocked to the floor. He lifts her up, and with his body crushes her against one of the glass doors. On the other side of it, there are hands, feet, a brain. She kisses him in anguish, solemnly.

Spanel wraps her legs around his waist and holds on to his neck with her hands. He presses her harder against the glass. Then he penetrates her, grabs hold of her face and looks her straight in the eye. He moves slowly, doesn't avert his gaze. She becomes frantic, shakes her head, wants to break free. But he won't let her. He can feel her ragged breath, she's nearly in agony. When she stops writhing, he runs his hand along her skin, and he kisses her and continues to move slowly. It's then that Spanel screams, she screams as if the world didn't exist, she screams as if words had split in two and lost all meaning, she screams as if beneath this hell, there was another hell, one from which she didn't want to escape.

He gets dressed while Spanel, still naked, sits on the chair, smoking. She smiles, showing all her teeth.

El Perro is still looking in through the window. Spanel knows he's there, on the other side of the door, but she ignores him.

He leaves without saying goodbye.

19

He gets into his car and lights a cigarette. But before he starts the engine, his phone rings. It's his sister.

"Hello."

"Hi, Marcos. Where are you? I see buildings. Are you in the city?"

"I am. I had to run some errands."

"Why don't you come over for lunch then."

"I can't, I have to go in to work."

"Marcos, I know perfectly well that today is your day off. The woman who answered the phone at the plant told me. I haven't seen you in ages."

He'd rather see his sister than go back home to the female.

"I'll make special kidneys in a lemon and herb marinade. You'll be licking it off your fingers."

"I'm not eating meat, Marisa."

His sister looks at him with surprise and a bit of suspicion.

"You're not one of those veganoids now, are you?"

"It's for health reasons, my doctor suggested I stop eating meat. It's just for a while."

"Is everything okay? Don't scare me, Marcos."

"It's nothing serious. My cholesterol's a bit high, that's all."

"Well, I'll think of something. But come over, I want to see you."

It's not for health reasons. Since his son died he hasn't gone back to eating meat.

The prospect of seeing his sister weighs on him. Visiting her is an errand to be taken care of when he has no other choice. He doesn't know who his sister is, not really.

He drives slowly through the city. There are people around, but it seems deserted. It's not just because the population has been reduced. Ever since animals were eliminated, there's been a silence that nobody hears, and yet it's there, always, resounding throughout the city. It's a shrill silence that can be seen on people's faces, in their gestures, in the way they look at one another. It's as if everyone's lives have been detained, as if they were waiting for the nightmare to end.

He arrives at his sister's place and gets out of the car. Somewhat resigned, he rings the doorbell.

"Hi, Marquitos!"

His sister's words are like boxes filled with blank paper. She gives him a hug that's limp, quick.

"Let me take your umbrella."

"I don't have one."

"Are you crazy? What do you mean you don't have one?"

"I don't have one, Marisa. I live out in the country and the birds won't do anything. It's only in the city that people are paranoid."

"Hurry up and come inside, will you."

His sister pushes him into the house and looks around. She's worried that the neighbours will see her brother without an umbrella.

He knows that what will ensue is the ritual of talking about trivialities, during which Marisa insinuates that she can't take responsibility for their father, and he says that she doesn't have to worry, and sees the two strangers that are her children, and she drops the guilt for six months until the whole thing repeats itself.

They go to the kitchen.

"How are you, Marquitos?"

He hates it when she calls him Marquitos. She does it to express a modicum of affection, which she doesn't feel.

"I'm fine."

"A bit better?"

There's pity and condescension in her eyes. It's the only way she's looked at him since he lost his son.

He doesn't answer, restricts himself to lighting a cigarette.

"I'm sorry but not in here, okay? You'll fill the house with the smell of smoke."

His sister's words accumulate, one on top of the other, like folders piled on folders inside folders. He puts out the cigarette.

He wants to leave.

"The food's ready. I'm just waiting to hear from Esteban."

Esteban is his sister's husband. Whenever he thinks of his brother-in-law, he sees a man hunched over, with a face full of contradictions and a half-smile that's an attempt at hiding them. He believes Esteban is a man trapped by his circumstances, by a wife who's a monument to stupidity and by a life he regrets having chosen.

"Oh, Esteban just got back to me. That's too bad. He has a lot of work and won't be able to make it."

"That's fine."

"The kids will be home soon from school."

His sister's kids. There are two of them. He thinks that she was never much interested in maternity, that she had her kids because it's one of the things you're supposed to do in life, like throwing a party on your fifteenth birthday, getting married, renovating your home and eating meat.

He says nothing because he doesn't care to see them. She serves him lemonade with mint in it and puts a plate below the glass. He takes a sip and puts it back down. The lemonade has an artificial taste.

"How are you, Marquitos? The truth."

She barely touches his hand and tilts her head, holding back the pity she feels, though not entirely, because she wants him to notice it. He looks at the fingers she's placed over his hand and thinks that not long ago, that hand grabbed hold of Spanel by the nape of her neck.

"I'm fine."

"How is it possible that you don't have an umbrella?"

He sighs a little and thinks that yet again, they're going to have the argument they do every year.

"I don't need one. Nobody needs one."

"Everyone needs one. There are areas that don't have protective roofs. Do you want to get yourself killed?"

"Marisa, do you seriously think that if a bird shits on your head, you're going to die?"

"Yes."

"I'll say it again, Marisa, in the country, at the plant, no one uses an umbrella, no one would even think of using one. Wouldn't it make more sense to believe that if you get bitten by a mosquito, which could have bitten an animal before you, you might get the virus?"

"No, because the government says there's no risk with mosquitoes."

"The government wants to manipulate you, that's the only reason it exists."

"Here everyone uses an umbrella when they go out. It's only logical."

"Have you ever stopped to think that maybe the umbrella industry saw an opportunity and the government got in on it?"

"You always think there's some conspiracy when there isn't."

He can hear her tapping the floor with her foot. Slowly, almost without making a sound, but he knows his sister has reached her limit, that she's incapable of discussing the subject further, more than anything because she doesn't think for herself. That's why she can't back up her point of view for very long.

"Let's not argue, Marquitos."

"Fine by me."

She uses her fingers to display the virtual screen on the kitchen table. In the menu, a photo of her children appears. She touches it and a window pops up. It shows her two kids, who are almost teenagers, walking down the street with air umbrellas.

"How much longer will you be?"

"We're almost there."

She closes the virtual screen and looks nervously at her brother. She doesn't know what to talk about.

"Those umbrellas were gifts from their grandparents, you have no idea how much they spoil the kids. They'd been asking for them for years, but they're so expensive. Who would think of making an umbrella with an air propeller? But the kids are happy, they're the envy of all their classmates."

He doesn't say anything and looks at a picture frame on the kitchen wall. The frame projects images of cheap still-life compositions. Fruits in baskets, oranges on a table, a series of unsigned drawings. Close to the frame he sees a cockroach on the wall. The cockroach crawls down to the countertop and disappears behind a plate of bread.

"The kids just love this virtual game their grandparents got them. It's called *My Real Pet*."

He doesn't ask her anything. His sister's words smell of detained humidity, of confinement, of intense cold. She keeps talking.

"You create your own animal and you can actually pet it, play with it, feed it. Mine's a white angora cat called Mishi. But she's just a kitten because I don't want her to get any bigger. I prefer baby cats, like everyone does."

He never liked cats. Or baby cats. He takes a sip of lemonade, hides his disgust and watches the images change in the picture frame. A still life flickers and then becomes pixelated. The frame goes black.

"The kids created a dragon and a unicorn. But we know they're going to get bored soon, just like they did with Boby, he was a robot dog we bought them. We saved up for so long and after a few months they got tired of him. Boby's in the garage, turned off. He's really well-made, but it's not the same thing as a real dog."

His sister always makes sure he understands that they don't have a lot of money, that theirs is an austere life. He knows this isn't true though he doesn't care either way, and doesn't hold a grudge because she contributes nothing, not even a penny, towards their father's care.

"I put together a warm salad with vegetables and rice for you. Does that sound okay?"

"Yes."

He notices a door near the sink that he doesn't remember. It's the kind of door found in households that raise heads. He can tell it's new and hasn't been used. Behind the door is a cold room. Now he understands why his sister invited him over. She's going to ask for heads at a good price so she can raise them.

They hear sounds from the street and the kids come in.

20

The kids are twins. A girl and a boy. They barely speak and when they do, it's to each other in whispers, using secret codes and words with meanings that are only implied. He looks at them as though they were a strange animal made up of two separate parts activated by a single mind. His sister insists on calling them "the kids", when everyone else refers to them as "the twins". His sister and her idiotic rules.

The twins sit down at the dining-room table without saying hello.

"You didn't say hi to Uncle Marquitos."

He gets up from the kitchen table and walks slowly to the dining room. What he wants is for the formality to be over, to end this obligatory visit as soon as possible.

"Hi, Uncle Marquitos."

They say this in unison, mechanically, imitating a robot. They hold in their laughter, which shows in their eyes. They stare at him without blinking, waiting for a reaction. But he sits down on a chair and pours himself some water, doesn't pay them any attention.

His sister serves the meal without noticing anything. She takes away his glass of water and replaces it with lemonade. "You forgot this in the kitchen, Marquitos. I made it just for you."

Though the twins aren't identical, their sealed and unwavering bond gives them an ominous air. The unconscious gestures that are duplicated, the identical gaze, the pacts of silence, make others uncomfortable. He knows they have a secret language, one it's unlikely even his sister can decipher. The words that only the two of them understand turn others into foreigners, strangers, make them illiterate. His sister's children are also a cliché: the evil twins.

His sister serves him the meatless food. It's cold. Flavourless.

"Is it good?"

"Yes."

The twins eat the special kidneys prepared with lemon and herbs, the potatoes à la provençale and the peas. They savour the meat while they look at him with curiosity. He sees the boy, Estebancito, gesture to the girl, Maru. He always laughs at the thought of the catastrophic dilemma his sister would have found herself in if she'd had two girls or two boys. Naming children after their parents is stripping them of an identity, reminding them who they belong to.

The twins laugh, give each other signs, whisper. The hair on both of their heads is dirty, or oily.

"Kids, we're having lunch with your uncle. Don't be rude. Your father and I talked to you about this. At the table we don't whisper, we talk like adults, understood?"

Estebancito looks at him with a sparkle in his eyes, a sparkle full of words like woods of splintered trees and silent tornadoes. But it's Maru who speaks. "We're trying to guess what Uncle Marquitos tastes like."

His sister takes her knife and stabs it into the table. The sound is furious, swift. "Enough," she says slowly, weighing the word, controlling it. The twins look at her with surprise. He's never seen his sister react this way. He looks at her silently and chews a bit more of his cold rice, feeling sad about the whole scene.

"I've had it with this game. We don't eat people. Or are the two of you savages?"

She shouts the question. Then she looks at the knife stuck in the table and runs to the toilet, as though awaking from a trance.

Maru, or Marisita, as his sister calls her, looks at the piece of special kidney she's about to put in her mouth, and with a hint of a smile, winks at her brother. His niece's words are like pieces of glass melting in extreme heat, like ravens pecking out eyes in slow motion.

"Mum's crazy."

She says this in the voice of a little girl, pouting and moving her index finger in circles near her temple.

Estebancito looks at her and laughs. He appears to find everything highly comical. He says, "The game's called *Exquisite Corpse*. Want to play?"

His sister comes back. She looks at him, embarrassed, somewhat resigned. "I apologize," she says. "It's a game that's popular now and they don't understand they're not allowed to play it."

He drinks some water. She keeps talking and it's like she figures he wants an explanation he hasn't asked for.

"The problem is social media and those little virtual groups they're part of, that's where these things get started. You have no idea because you're never online."

She notices the knife is still stuck in the table and yanks it out quickly as if nothing had happened, as if she hadn't overreacted.

He knows that if he gets up and leaves as though he's been offended, he'll have to go through the whole thing again soon, because his sister will ask him over as many times as are needed to apologize. Instead, he restricts himself to saying, "I think Estebancito must taste a bit rancid, like a pig that's been fattened for too long, and Maru not unlike pink salmon, a bit on the strong side, but delicious."

At first the twins look at him without understanding. They've never had pork or salmon. Then they smile, amused. His sister looks at him and doesn't say anything. She's only able to take another sip of water and eat. Her words get stuck inside her as though trapped in vacuum packed plastic bags.

"So tell me, Marquitos, does the plant sell heads to individual households, to someone like myself?"

He swallows what he believes to be vegetables. He can't tell what he's eating, not by its colour nor its flavour. There's a sour smell in the air. It could be his food or the house.

"Are you listening to me?"

He looks at her for a few seconds without answering. It occurs to him that since he got there, she hasn't asked him about their father.

"No."

"That's not what the secretary at the plant said."

He decides it's time to end the visit.

"Dad's fine, Marisa, in case you were wondering."

She lowers her eyes and recognizes the sign that her brother has had enough.

"That's wonderful."

"Yes, it is wonderful."

But he decides to take it further because she crossed a line when she called the plant to ask about things she shouldn't have.

"He had an episode a little while ago."

His sister leaves her fork suspended in the air, halfway to her mouth, as though she were genuinely surprised.

"He did?"

"Yes. He's doing fine, but it does happen from time to time."

"Right, of course."

He points to his niece and nephew with his fork and, raising his voice a little, says, "Have the kids, his grandchildren, gone to visit him?"

His sister looks at him with surprise and contained fury. Their tacit contract implies not humiliating her, and he's always respected it. Until today.

"Between school, homework, how far away he is, it's really tough. And then there's the curfew."

Maru is about to say something, but her mother touches her hand and keeps talking.

"You have to understand that they're enrolled in the best school—it's an excellent school, a state school, of course, because private schools are terribly expensive. But if they don't keep up, they'll have to transfer to one with a fee and that's not something we can take on."

His sister's words are like dry leaves piled up in a corner, rotting.

"Of course, Marisa. I'll send Dad regards from everyone, okay?"

He gets up and smiles at his niece and nephew, but doesn't say goodbye.

Maru gives him a defiant look. She takes a bite of special kidney and says, her mouth open, almost shouting: "I wanna go visit Grandpa, Mum."

Estebancito looks at her, amused, and follows this up with: "Come on, Mum, let's go visit, can't we go visit."

His sister looks at them with confusion; she doesn't pick up on the cruelty of the request, doesn't see the suppressed laughter.

"All right, all right, I guess we can go."

He knows he won't see the twins for a long time, and he knows that if he were to cut an arm off each of his sister's children and eat them at this very moment on the wooden table, they would taste exactly like he predicted. He looks them right in the eye. First Maru and then Estebancito. He looks at his niece and nephew as though he were savouring the taste of them. It startles them and they lower their eyes.

He walks straight to the door. His sister opens it and gives him a quick kiss goodbye.

"So great to see you, Marquitos. Take this umbrella, do me a favour."

He opens the umbrella and leaves without answering. Before he gets into his car he sees a bin. He tosses the open umbrella into it. His sister is watching from the door. She closes it slowly while lowering her head.

21

He drives to the abandoned zoo.

Lunch with his sister always puts him on edge. Not to such an extent that he stops going, but he feels the need to collect himself afterwards, in order to understand why this person who's part of his family is the way she is, why she has the children she does, why she's never cared about him or their father.

He walks slowly past the monkey cages. They're broken. The trees that were planted inside them have dried up. He reads one of the signs, its letters discoloured:

Howler monkey
Alouatta caraya
Class: Mammals

Next to the word "Mammals", there's an obscene drawing.

Order: Primates
Family: Atelidae
Habitat: Woods
Adaptations: The females have golden or yellowish fur, while that of the male

The words that follow are worn away.

They have special features that enable them to produce sounds. Their larynx and hyoid bone in particular are highly developed, the latter forming a large capsule that amplifies their vocalizations.
Diet: Plants, insects and fruits
Conservation status: Out of danger

The words "Out of danger" have a cross through them.

Distribution: Central zone of South America, from eastern Bolivia and southern Brazil to northern Argentina and Paraguay

There's a photo of a male howler monkey. The monkey's face is contorted, as though the camera captured the moment it was caught. Someone has drawn a red circle with a cross in the centre.

He goes into one of the cages. There's grass growing up between cracks in the cement, cigarettes and needles on the floor. He finds bones, thinks they could be one of the monkeys'. Or not. They could be anything.

There are trees outside the cage, and he leaves it to walk beneath them. It's a hot day and the sky is clear. The trees provide a bit of shade. He's sweating.

He comes across a sales booth. When he sticks his head through the empty door frame, he finds cans, papers, filth. Inside, he reads the list of products painted on the wall: Simba the stuffed lion, Rita the stuffed giraffe, Dumbo the stuffed elephant, animal kingdom cup, tit monkey pencil case. The white walls are covered with graffiti, sentences, drawings. Someone has written "I miss the animals" in small, restrained letters. Someone else crossed the words out and added "I hope you die for being so dumb."

When he leaves the sales booth, he lights a cigarette. He never wanders around the zoo, but instead always goes straight to the lion's den and sits there. He knows the zoo is large because he remembers spending hours exploring it with his father.

He steps down into some empty swimming pools. The pools are small. They could have held otters, or seals, he thinks, but can't remember. The signs have been torn off.

As he walks, he rolls up his sleeves. He undoes the buttons on his shirt and leaves it open, loose.

In the distance, he sees huge cages, they're tall, topped with cupolas. He remembers the aviary. The colourful birds flying, the burst of feathers, the smell both dense and fragile. When he reaches the cages, he sees it's actually one cage, split into sections. Inside there's a large hanging bridge covered by a glass cupola, which once allowed visitors to walk among the birds. The doors are broken. The trees that were planted inside the cage grew up and broke through the glass cupolas over the roof and bridge. He steps on leaves and shards of glass, feels them crunch beneath his boots. There's a staircase up to the hanging bridge. He climbs it and decides to cross the bridge. He walks through branches, steps over them, pushes them out of his way. In a clearing, he looks up to the roof and sees the treetops and one of the cupolas, the one in the centre. It's the only one made of stained glass and has an image of a man with wings flying close to the sun. He recognizes Icarus, knows of his fate. The wings are made of different colours and Icarus is flying through a sky that's full of birds, as though they were keeping him company, as though this human were one of them. He picks up a branch with leaves on it and cleans the floor of the bridge a little so he can lie down without cutting himself on the glass. Some parts of the cupola are broken, but it's the least damaged of them all because it's the highest and furthest from the branches of the trees, which haven't yet reached it.

He wishes he could spend the whole day lying there looking up at the multicoloured sky. He would have liked to show this aviary to his son, just as it is, empty, broken. A memory strikes him of his sister's phone calls when Leo died. She only spoke to Cecilia, as though his wife were the only one who needed to be consoled. At the funeral, crying, she held on to her children as though she feared they too would die a sudden death, as though the baby in the casket had the ability to infect others with its fate. He looked at everyone as though the world had distanced itself a few metres; it was as though the people embracing him were behind frosted glass. He wasn't able to cry, not once, not even when he saw the small white coffin being lowered into the ground. What he was thinking was that he wished the coffin were less conspicuous; he knew it was white because of the purity of the child inside, but are we really that pure when we arrive in this world, he wondered. He thought of other lives, thought that maybe in another dimension, on another planet, in another era, he might find himself with his son and watch him grow. And while he was thinking about all this and people were throwing roses onto the coffin, his sister cried as though this child were her own.

Nor did he cry later, after the simulacrum of a funeral that was still expected back then. When the guests had left and the two of them remained, the cemetery employees lifted the coffin back up, wiped away the earth and flowers that had been thrown on it and took it into a room. They removed his son's body from the white coffin and placed it in one that was transparent. He and Cecilia had to watch their baby slowly enter the oven that would cremate him. Cecilia collapsed and was taken into another room with armchairs that was set up for this purpose. He received the ashes and signed the papers that verified that his son had been cremated and that they had witnessed it.

He leaves the aviary and walks past a kids' playground. The slide is broken. There's a seesaw that's missing one of its seats. The merry-go-round shaped like a spinning top has retained its green colour, but swastikas have been painted on its wooden floor. Grass is growing in the sandbox and someone has placed a rickety chair in the middle of it and left it there to rot. Only one swing is left. He sits down on it and lights a cigarette. The chains still hold his weight. He swings by moving his legs gently, his feet touching the ground. Then he starts to pump his legs, lifting his feet into the air, and sees that in the distance, clouds are forming in the sky.

It's a hot day. He takes off his shirt and ties it around his waist.

Not far from the playground he sees another cage. He goes over to it and reads the sign.

Sulphur-crested cockatoo
Cacatua galerita
Class: Aves
Order: Psittaciformes
Family: Psittacidae

Someone has written "I love you, Romina" in red letters over the description of the habitat.

Adaptations: The males have eyes the colour of dark coffee, while the females' eyes are red. During courtship, the male raises his crest and moves his head in the shape of an eight while he emits vocalizations. Both parents take responsibility for incubating and feeding the chicks. The bird lives to about 40 years of age in the wild and to almost 65 in captivity (there's a record of a cockatoo that lived to over 120).

The rest of the sign is broken and lying on the floor, but he doesn't bend down to pick it up.

He walks over to a large building. The door frame has been burned. The building contains a room with big windows that have been broken. He thinks the space must have been a bar or restaurant. There are built-in chairs that weren't removed. Most of the tables are gone but two remain soldered to the floor. There's an elongated structure that could have been a bar.

Then he sees a sign that says "Serpentarium", and an arrow. He walks through hallways that are dark and narrow until he reaches a bigger space with wide windows. There's another sign painted on the wall. It says: "Serpentarium, please wait in line." He goes into a room with a high ceiling, part of which is broken. The sky shows through the cracks. There are no cages. Instead, the walls are divided into compartments by glass panels. He thinks they're called terrariums. There were once different serpents inside them. Some of the glass panels are broken, others have disappeared completely.

He sits down on the floor and pulls out a cigarette. As he looks around at the graffiti and drawings, an image catches his attention. It's a mask that someone has drawn with a good deal of skill. It looks like a Venetian mask. Beside it, in large black letters, the person has written: "The mask of apparent calm, of mundane tranquillity, of the joy, at once small and bright, of not knowing when this thing I call skin will be ripped off, when this thing I call mouth will lose the flesh that surrounds it, when these things I call eyes will come upon the black silence of a knife." It's not signed. No one has scratched it out or drawn over it, but words and images surround it. He reads some of the things people have written: "black market", "why don't you rip this", "meat with a first and last name tastes best!", "joy? small and bright? seriously? LOL!", "awesome poem!!", "after the curfew we can eat you", "this world is shit", "YOLO", "Oh, eat of me, eat of my flesh / Oh, amongst cannibals / Oh, take your time to / cut me up / Oh, amongst cannibals / Soda Stereo forever."

As he's trying to remember what "YOLO" means, he hears a sound. He keeps still. It's a faint cry. He gets up and walks through the serpentarium to one of the largest windows. It's intact.

It's hard for him to make anything out. There are dry branches on the floor, filth. But he sees a body move. And then suddenly, a tiny head lifts up. It has a black snout and two brown ears. Then he makes out another head and another and another.

He stands there watching them, thinks he's hallucinating. Then he feels an urge to break the glass so he can touch them. At first, he doesn't understand how they got there, but then he realizes there are three terrariums connected by doors and that the glass surrounding two of them is broken. They're not on ground level, which is why he has to climb up to enter them. He gets down on all fours and crawls through the door to the largest terrarium, the one in the middle, which is where the puppies are. The door is open. The terrarium is wide and fairly tall. He thinks it would have held an anaconda, or a python. The puppies whimper, they're frightened. Of course, he thinks, they've never seen a human in their lives. He crawls along carefully because the floor is covered in stones, dry leaves, filth. The puppies are beneath some branches that do a fairly good job of sheltering them. Branches around which a boa might have wrapped itself, he thinks. They're curled up next to each other to keep warm and protect themselves. He sits down close by but doesn't touch them until they're calmer. Then he starts to pet the puppies. There are four of them, they're scrawny and filthy. They sniff at his hands. He picks one of them up. It hardly weighs a thing. At first it trembles, but then it begins to move desperately. It urinates out of fear. The others bark, whimper. He hugs the puppy, kisses it until it calms down. The puppy runs its tongue along his face. He laughs and cries silently.

22

With the puppies, he loses track of time. They play at attacking him, try to catch the branches he moves through the air. They nip at his hands with their tiny teeth and it almost tickles. He grabs their heads and shakes them carefully, as if his hand were the jaw of a monstrous beast who was after them. He tugs gently on their tails. When they whimper and bark, he does too. They lick his hands. All four of the puppies are males.

He gives them names: Jagger, Watts, Richards and Wood.

The puppies run around the terrarium. Jagger bites Richards's tail. Wood appears to be asleep but gets up suddenly, grabs one of the branches with his mouth and shakes it in the air. But Watts is mistrustful, and sniffs at this man in the terrarium, then plays around him, smells him and barks, before climbing up his legs with clumsy movements. He attacks Watts, and the puppy cries a little and nips him on the hand, his tail wagging. Then Watts jumps onto Richards and Jagger. He attacks the other puppies but then they chase after him.

He thinks of his dogs. Pugliese and Koko. He had had to slaughter them knowing, suspecting, that the virus was a lie invented by global powers and legitimized by the government and media. He'd considered abandoning his dogs to avoid having to kill them, but he was afraid they'd be tortured. Keeping them could have been much worse.

They could have all been tortured. Back then, injections were sold to prevent pets from suffering. They were for sale everywhere, even at the supermarket. He buried Pugliese and Koko beneath the biggest tree in the yard. The three of them would sit under its shade on afternoons when the heat was intense and he didn't have to work at his father's processing plant. While he sipped on a beer and read, they were by his side. He'd bring his father's old handheld radio and listen to a programme that played instrumental jazz. He enjoyed the ritual of having to tune in to the station. Every so often, Pugliese would get up and chase after a bird. Koko would raise her head, drowsy with sleep, and look first at Pugliese, then at him, in a way that he always thought meant, "Pugliese is mad, stark raving mad. But we love him just as he is, bonkers," and he'd always pet her head, smiling and saying softly, "Sweet Taylor, my beautiful Koko." But when his father came by, Koko was a different dog. She couldn't contain her happiness. Something lit up inside her, a dormant engine, and she began to jump, run, wag her tail, bark. When she saw him, no matter how far away he was, she'd bolt in his direction and jump on him. He always greeted her with a smile, hugged her, picked her up. Koko would wag her tail differently for his father, that was how he knew his dad was near. She only did this for the man who had found her on the side of the highway, curled up and dirty, a few weeks old, dehydrated, on the verge of death. His father had kept Koko by his side twenty-four hours a day; he'd taken her to the plant and looked after her until she began to respond. He thinks that slaughtering

Koko was another of the reasons for his father's mental collapse.

Suddenly the four puppies go quiet and perk up their ears. He becomes tense. At no point has the obvious occurred to him. The puppies have a mother.

He hears a growl. On the other side of the glass, two dogs are baring their fangs. It takes him less than a second to react. In this instant, he thinks he'd like to die here, in this terrarium, with these puppies. That way at least his body could serve as food and these animals could live a little longer. But then the image of his father in the nursing home comes to him, and so quickly it's instinctive, he drags himself to the door through which he entered. He pushes the door shut and locks it. The dogs are already on the other side, barking, scratching, trying to get in. If he leaves the door locked and escapes through the one that connects to the adjoining terrarium, the puppies will die. But if he opens this door with the puppies inside, he won't have time to escape before the dogs attack. The door to the adjoining terrarium is closed. He tries to open it but can't. The puppies are whimpering. They curl up to protect themselves. He decides to cover them with his shirt, though he knows it won't keep them safe. He lies down on the floor in front of the door he intends to leave through and starts to kick it. After several kicks, the door gives. He breathes. The dogs bark and paw at the glass more forcefully. He makes sure that the door leading to the adjoining terrarium is completely open and knows he'll be able to escape that way because the glass is broken. The growling intensifies. He thinks there are now more dogs.

Either that or those already out there are getting more enraged by the second.

The puppies are curled up, confused, poking their tiny heads out from under his shirt. He picks up a medium-sized stone and props it against the locked door, the one the pack is trying to get in through. Then he unlocks it. He knows that eventually the dogs will be able to push it open, though it'll be difficult. He finds another stone that's a little bigger and, on all fours, drags it to the adjoining terrarium. He jams the door in place with the large stone because his kicks destroyed the latch. Then he leaves through the broken glass, carefully, without jumping or making any loud noises. When he's on the ground floor, he starts to run.

He runs without stopping or looking back. The sky is heavy with dark clouds, but he doesn't notice. It's when he sees his car that he hears the barking more clearly. He turns his head slightly and sees a pack of dogs getting closer and closer. He runs as though it were the last thing he was going to do on earth. Seconds before the dogs reach him, he's in his car. When he catches his breath, he looks at them sadly because he can't help them, because he can't feed them, wash them, take care of them, hug them. He counts six dogs. They're scrawny, probably malnourished. He's not afraid, though he knows they could tear him apart if he got out of the car. He can't stop looking at them. It's been a long time since he's seen an animal. The alpha male, the leader of the pack, is a black dog. The six of them surround the car, barking, dirtying the windows with white froth from their snouts, pawing at the closed doors. He looks at the fangs, the hunger, the fury. They're beautiful, he thinks. He doesn't want to hurt them. They follow him until he presses the accelerator, and in his mind he says goodbye to Jagger, Watts, Richards and Wood.

23

As he pulls up to his house, he misses the way Koko and Pugliese used to bark and chase after the car along the dirt road lined with eucalyptus trees. It was Koko who had found Pugliese. He was crying under the tree where the two of them are now buried. He was a puppy only a few months old, full of fleas and ticks, and malnourished. Koko adopted him as if he were her own. And though he'd been the one who removed the fleas and ticks from the pup, and fed him so he'd regain strength, Pugliese always saw Koko as his saviour. If someone shouted at Koko or threatened her, Pugliese went crazy. He was a loyal dog who looked out for everyone, but Koko was his favourite.

The sky is loaded down with black clouds, but he doesn't notice them. He gets out of the car and walks straight to the barn. The female is there. Curled up, asleep. He has to wash her, it can't wait. He looks around the barn and thinks that he should clean it, create a space in which the female can be more comfortable.

When he leaves to get a bucket to clean her, it starts to rain. It's only then that he realizes a storm is coming, one of those summer storms that's both frightening and beautiful.

He goes into the kitchen and feels a crushing exhaustion. What he wants to do is sit down and have a beer, but he can't put off cleaning the female any longer. He gets the bucket, a bar of white soap and a clean rag. In the bathroom, he looks around for an old comb without much luck, until eventually he finds the one Cecilia left behind, and picks it up. He thinks he'll have to connect the hose, but when he's back outside, it's raining so hard he gets soaked. His shirt is with Jagger, Watts, Richards and Wood. He takes off his boots and socks. All he has on are his jeans.

Barefoot, he walks over to the barn. He feels the wet grass beneath his feet, smells the wet earth. He sees Pugliese barking at the rain. Sees the dog as though he were there, at that moment. Crazy Pugliese jumping around, trying to catch the drops, getting covered in mud, seeking the approval of Koko, who always looked out for him from the porch.

Carefully, almost tenderly, he takes the female out of the barn. The rain frightens her and she tries to cover herself. He calms her down, pets her head and, as though she could understand, says, "Don't worry, it's just water, it'll clean you up." He soaps the female's hair and she looks at him with terror. To reassure her, he sits her down in the grass. Then he gets on his knees behind her. Her hair, which he moves around clumsily, fills with white soap suds. He goes slowly, he doesn't want to frighten her. The female blinks and moves her head to look at him in the rain, she writhes, trembles.

The rain falls hard and starts to clean her. He soaps her arms and rubs them with the clean rag. The female is calmer now, but she looks at him with a degree of distrust. He soaps her back and then slowly brings her to her feet. Now he cleans her chest, armpits, stomach. Diligently, as though he were cleaning a valuable, but inanimate object. He's nervous, as if the object could break, or come to life.

With the rag, he wipes off the initials that certify the female is First Generation Pure. There are twenty of them, one for each of her years in the breeding centre.

Then he moves on to her face, and with his hand, cleans the dirt stuck to it. He notices her long eyelashes and her eyes, which are a vague colour. They're perhaps grey, or green. She has a few scattered freckles.

He crouches down to clean her feet, calves, thighs. Even with the drops of rain falling hard, he can smell her, wild and fresh, the scent of jasmine. With the comb in his hand, he sits her back down in the grass. Then he moves behind her and begins to work it through her hair. She has straight hair, but it's tangled. He has to comb it carefully so he doesn't hurt her.

When he's finished, he brings her to her feet and looks at her. There, in the rain, he sees her. As fragile, as nearly translucent, as perfect. He moves towards the smell of jasmine, and without thinking, hugs her. The female doesn't move or tremble. She just raises her head and looks at him. Her eyes are green, he thinks, definitely green. He runs his hand over the mark on her forehead where she's been branded. Then he kisses it, because he knows she suffered when they did it to her, just as she suffered when they removed her vocal cords so she'd be more submissive, so she wouldn't scream when she was slaughtered. He strokes her neck. Now, he's the one who trembles. He removes his jeans and stands there, naked. His breath quickens. He continues to hug her as it rains down.

What he wants to do is prohibited. But he does it anyway.

TWO

...like a caged beast born of caged beasts born of caged beasts born of caged beasts born in a cage and dead in a cage, born and then dead, born in a cage and then dead in a cage, in a word like a beast, in one of their words, like such a beast...

SAMUEL BECKETT

1

When he wakes, his body is covered in a film of sweat. It's not hot outside, not yet, not during the spring. He goes to the kitchen and pours himself some water. Then he turns on the TV, presses the mute button and flips through the channels without paying attention. Eventually he stops on a channel that's replaying old news, from years ago. People had started vandalizing urban sculptures of animals. The programme shows a group of individuals throwing paint, rubbish and eggs at the Wall Street Bull. Then it cuts to other images, a crane raising the bronze sculpture that weighs more than 3,000 kilograms, the bull moving through the air while people look on in horror, point at it, cover their mouths. He switches the mute button off but keeps the volume low. Isolated attacks had taken place in museums. Someone had slashed Klee's *Cat and Bird* at the MoMA. The news anchor discusses experts' efforts to restore the painting. At the Museo del Prado, a woman had tried to destroy Goya's *Cats Fighting* with her own hands. She'd lunged at it but the security guards stopped her in time. He remembers the experts, art historians, curators, critics who were indignant and spoke of the "regression to medieval times", of the return to an "iconoclastic society". He drinks some water and turns off the TV.

Then he remembers the sculptures of San Francisco de Asís that were burned, the donkeys, sheep, dogs, camels removed from nativity scenes, the sculptures of sea lions in Mar del Plata that were destroyed.

He can't sleep and has to be up early to meet a member of the Church of the Immolation. There are more and more of them, he thinks. The calm and orderly pace of the slaughter is disrupted whenever the lunatics from the church stop by the plant. This week he has to go to the game reserve and the laboratory. Tasks that take him away from home, that complicate matters. He has to get them done but lately he hasn't been able to concentrate. Though Krieg hasn't talked to him about it, he knows his work has suffered.

With his eyes closed, he tries to count his breaths. But then he feels something touch him and jumps. He opens his eyes and sees her. Then he moves over and she lies down on the sofa. He inhales her wild, vibrant smell, hugs her. "Hi, Jasmine." He untied her when he woke up.

He turns the TV back on. She likes to look at the images. At first she was afraid of it, and tried repeatedly to break it. The sounds were grating, the images put her on edge. But as the days passed, she understood that the device couldn't hurt her, that what occurred inside it wouldn't do anything to her, and she became fascinated by the images. Everything was a source of surprise. Water coming out of the tap, the new, delicious food that was so different from the balanced feed, the music on the radio, taking showers in the bathroom, the furniture, walking freely through the house while he was around to keep an eye on her.

He straightens her nightgown. Getting her to wear clothes was a task that required a huge amount of patience.

She ripped her dresses, pulled them off, urinated on them. Far from getting angry, he was amazed at the strength of her character, at her tenacity. Over time, she understood that the clothes covered her up, that in a way, they protected her. She also learnt to dress herself.

She looks at him and points to the TV. She laughs. He does too, without knowing what he's laughing at, or why, but he does it anyway, and pulls her a little closer. Jasmine doesn't make any sounds, but her smile vibrates throughout her body and he finds it infectious.

He runs his hand over her belly. She's eight months pregnant.

2

He has to get going, but first he wants to have some *mate* with Jasmine. The water's already been heated on the stove. It took him a lot of time to get her to understand the concept of fire, its dangers and uses. Whenever he lit the burner, she took off and ran to the other end of the house. Her fear turned into wonder. Then all she wanted to do was touch the white and blue that could sometimes be yellow, that seemed to dance, that was alive. She'd touch the flames until they burned her and then pull her hand away quickly, frightened. She'd suck on her fingers and step back a little, but then she'd move closer and do it again and again. Slowly, fire became part of her daily life, her new reality.

When he's had one last sip of *mate*, he kisses her, and as he does every day, walks her to the room where he keeps her locked up. He turns the bolt in the front door and gets into his car. She'll be fine watching the TV he mounted on the wall, sleeping, drawing with the crayons he left her, eating the food he made for her, flipping through the pages of books she doesn't understand. He wishes he could teach her to read, but what's the point if she can't speak and will never be part of a society that sees her only as an edible product? The mark on her forehead, the huge, clear, indestructible mark, forces him to keep her locked up in the house.

He drives to the plant quickly. He intends to get what needs to be done over with and go back home. But his phone rings. He sees it's Cecilia and pulls over to the side of the road. She's been calling more often lately. He's afraid she wants to come home. There's no way he can tell her what's going on. She wouldn't understand. He's been trying to avoid her, but that's just made it worse. She can feel his impatience, sees that the pain has become something else. She says, "You're different"; "Your face has changed"; "Why didn't you pick up the other day, are you that busy?"; "You've already forgotten about me, about us." The "us" she refers to isn't limited to her and him, it includes Leo, but saying so out loud would be cruel.

When he arrives at the plant, he nods to the security guard and parks his car. He doesn't care whether the man is reading the paper, doesn't even bother to check who he is. He no longer stops for a smoke, his arms propped up on the car roof. What he does is go straight to Krieg's office. He gives Mari a quick kiss on the cheek, and she says: "Hi, Marcos. You're really late, love. Señor Krieg is downstairs. The people from that church are here and he's gone to deal with them." This last part she says with annoyance. "They're showing up more and more often." He doesn't say anything, though he knows he is late and what's more that the people from the church were early. He goes downstairs quickly and runs through the hallways without greeting the workers on the way.

The lobby is where they meet suppliers and people who don't work at the plant. Krieg is standing there, not saying a thing, swaying slowly, almost imperceptibly, as though he had no choice. He looks uncomfortable. In front of him, there's a delegation of about ten people. They're dressed in white tunics and their heads are shaved. They watch Krieg in silence. One of them wears a red tunic.

He goes up to them and shakes the hand of each one. Then he apologizes for being late. Krieg says that Marcos, the manager, will now look after them, and excuses himself to take a phone call.

Krieg walks away quickly without looking back, as though the members of the church were contagious. He runs his hands over his trousers, cleansing himself of something that could be sweat, or rage.

Once Krieg is gone, he goes up to the man he recognizes as the spiritual master, which is what they call the leader, and holds out his hand. He asks the man for the papers that permit and certify the sacrifice. He looks them over and sees that everything is in order. The spiritual master tells him that the church member who will be immolated has been examined by a doctor and has prepared his testament and performed his departure ritual. The man gives him another piece of paper that's been stamped and certified by a notary and says, "I, Gastón Schafe, authorize my body to be used as food for other people," and contains a signature and ID number. Gastón Schafe steps forward in his red tunic. He's a seventy-year-old man.

Gastón Schafe smiles and recites the Church of the Immolation's creed passionately and with conviction: "The human being is the cause of all evil in this world. We are our own virus."

All of the church members raise their hands and shout "Virus."

Gastón Schafe continues, "We are the worst kind of vermin, destroying our planet, starving our fellow man."

He's interrupted again. "Fellow man," shout the church members.

"My life will truly take on meaning once my body feeds another human being, one who truly needs it. Why waste my protein value in a meaningless cremation? I've lived my life, that's good enough for me."

In unison, all the church members shout, "Save the planet, immolate yourself!"

A few months back, a young woman had been chosen for sacrifice. In the middle of the church's discourse, Mari came downstairs shouting. A young woman committing suicide was an atrocity, she said, no one was saving the planet, the whole thing was nonsense, she wouldn't allow a bunch of lunatics to brainwash a woman so young, they should be embarrassed, maybe consider mass suicide, and if they really wanted to help, why didn't they donate all their organs. A Church of the Immolation whose members were alive was utterly grotesque, she shouted, until finally he wrapped his arms around her and took her to another room. He sat Mari down and gave her a glass of water and waited until she was calm. She cried a little and then composed herself. "Why don't they just give themselves to the black market, why do they have to come here?" Mari asked him, her face contorted.

"Because they need things to be legal so the church can remain in operation, they need the certificates."

Krieg let the incident go because he agreed with everything she'd said.

The plant is under obligation to deal with the church and "go through the whole grim ordeal", as Mari puts it. None of the processing plants wanted anything to do with them. The church fought for years until the government gave in and the two sides signed an agreement. Their success occurred only after the addition of a member who had high-ranking contacts and a lot of means. Eventually the government came to an arrangement with a few processing plants that now deal with the church members. In exchange, they're given tax breaks. That eliminated the problem of a group of lunatics who jeopardized the whole false structure built around the legitimization of cannibalism. If a person with a first and last name can be eaten legally, and they're not considered a product, what's stopping anyone from eating anyone else? But the government didn't stipulate what was to be done with the meat because it's meat no one wants to consume, not if they know where it comes from and have to pay market value for it. A while back, Krieg made a call when it came to the Church of the Immolation. The sacrificed person's meat would be given a special certificate for consumption by those most in need, with no further explanation. The members take this certificate and file it away along with the others they've been given over the years. The reality is that the meat really does go to those most in need, the Scavengers, who are already lurking close to the fence. Because they know a feast awaits them. It doesn't matter if it's old meat, for them it's a delicacy because it's fresh.

But the problem with the Scavengers is that they're marginalized and society regards them as being of no value. That's why the immolated person can't be told their body will be disembowelled, torn apart, chewed up and devoured by an outcast, an undesirable.

He gives the church members time to say goodbye to the person who's about to be sacrificed, to Gastón Schafe, who appears to be in a state of ecstasy. He knows it won't last long: when they reach the box sector, Gastón Schafe will probably vomit, or cry, or want to escape, or wet himself. Those who don't are either heavily drugged or severely psychotic. He's aware that the plant's employees have placed bets. While he waits for the hugs to end, he wonders what Jasmine is doing. At first he had to leave her locked up in the barn so she wouldn't hurt herself or destroy the house. He asked Krieg for the holiday he hadn't taken and spent several weeks at home, teaching her how to live in a house, how to sit down at the table for dinner, how to hold a fork, how to clean herself, how to pick up a glass of water, how to open a fridge, how to use the toilet. He had to teach her not to feel fear. Fear that was learnt, ingrained, accepted.

Gastón Schafe steps forward and raises his hands in front of him. He gives himself over with dramatic gestures, as though the whole ritual had some value. He recites, "As Jesus said, Take and eat of my body."

Listening to Gastón Schafe's triumphant voice, he's the only one who sees the decadence to the whole scene.

The decadence and the insanity.

He waits for the rest of the group to leave. A security guard walks them to the exit. "Carlitos, see them out," he tells the guard, with a gesture that Carlitos knows means, "See them out and make sure they don't return."

He asks Gastón Schafe to take a seat and offers him a glass of water. The heads are required to undergo a complete fast before slaughter, but the rules don't matter here. This meat is for the Scavengers, who don't care about subtleties, or norms, or violations. His objective is for the man to be as calm as possible, given the circumstances. He goes to get the glass of water and speaks to Carlitos, who confirms that the church members have left. They all got into a white van and he saw them drive away.

Gastón Schafe takes the glass of water, unaware that it contains a tranquillizer, a weak one, but one that's strong enough to ensure the man's reaction will be as minimal and non-violent as possible when they reach the boxes. He started using the tranquillizers fairly recently, after a situation arose with the young woman about to be sacrificed. The whole plant had been involved. It had happened on the day he'd learnt that Jasmine was pregnant. That morning, he'd given her a home pregnancy test after noticing that in addition to not menstruating, she'd gained a bit of weight. At first, he'd felt happiness, or something like it. Then it was fear he felt. Then confusion. What was he going to do? The baby couldn't be his, not officially, not if he didn't want them to take it away, put it in a breeding centre and send Jasmine and himself straight to the Municipal Slaughterhouse. He hadn't planned on going in to work that day, but Mari had called and said it was urgent: "That church is here, the Immolation Church, they're driving me crazy, they changed the date on me and now they're here and telling me I'm the one who made a mistake. And Krieg's not here and I'm not about to deal with them. Just imagine, Marcos, I want to shake them to their senses, they're all crazy, I can't even look at them." He hung up and drove to the plant. But he couldn't think of anything other than the baby, his child. The child that was really his. He'd come up with something to ensure no one took it away. When he got to the plant, he was impatient with the church members. That Claudia Ramos, the woman about to be sacrificed, was young, didn't matter to him. He didn't think to have someone see the church members to the exit, and took Claudia Ramos straight to the boxes. Nor did it matter to him that she was looking through the windows into the offal and slitting rooms and that with each step was becoming increasingly pale and nervous. He didn't take into account that Sergio was on break and that Ricardo, the less-experienced stunner, was working. Nor did he think twice when they entered the box sector's lounge and Ricardo grabbed her arm as though she were an animal. Ricardo tried to remove her tunic so she'd be naked for stunning and was somewhat violent and disrespectful with her. Claudia Ramos broke free, frightened, and ran off. She ran desperately through the plant, from room to room, shouting, "I don't wanna die, I don't wanna die," until she reached the unloading sector and saw a lot of heads coming down from the trucks. She went straight for them yelling, "No, don't kill us, please, no, don't kill us, don't kill us." He looked on as Sergio, who had seen her approaching at full speed, and knew she was from the Church of the Immolation because heads don't talk, grabbed his club (which he was never without) and stunned her with such precision that they were all amazed. He'd run after Claudia Ramos, but hadn't been able to catch her. When he saw Sergio stun her, he breathed a sigh of relief. Then he called security on his walkie-talkie and asked if the church members had left. "Just now," the guard answered. It was then that he ordered two workers to take the woman to the Scavenger sector. An unconscious Claudia Ramos was cut to pieces with machetes and knives, and devoured by the Scavengers lurking nearby, metres away from the electric fence. Krieg learnt of what had happened but didn't give the incident much thought; as the owner of the plant, he'd had it with the church. But unlike Krieg, he understood that it couldn't happen again, that if Sergio hadn't stunned her, it could have been worse.

Gastón Schafe stumbles a little. The tranquillizer has taken effect. They pass the offal and slitting rooms, but the windows are covered. Then they're at the boxes. Sergio is waiting for them at the door. Gastón Schafe is a little pale, but he's keeping it together. Sergio takes off his tunic and shoes. Gastón Schafe is now naked. He trembles a little and looks around, confused. He's about to speak, but Sergio grabs his arm carefully, and blindfolds him. Sergio guides Gastón Schafe into the box. The man moves desperately, says something that's not clear. As he watches Sergio handle Gastón Schafe, he thinks they'll have to increase the dose of the tranquillizer. Sergio adjusts the stainless steel shackle around the man's neck and talks to him. He seems to calm down, or at least stop moving and talking. Sergio raises the club and hits him on the forehead. Gastón

Schafe falls. Two workers pick him up and take him to the Scavenger sector.

The electric fence can't silence the cries and the sound of the machetes slicing open his body, the Scavengers fighting for the best piece of Gastón Schafe.

3

He gets home tired. Before opening Jasmine's room, he takes a shower, otherwise she won't let him do so in peace. She'll try to get under the water with him, kiss him, hug him. He understands she's alone all day, that when he gets home she wants to follow him around the house.

He opens the door and Jasmine greets him with a hug. He forgets about Gastón Schafe, Mari and the boxes.

There are mattresses on the floor. The room contains no furniture within reach; nothing that could hurt her. He set it up this way when he found out she was pregnant. He didn't want to risk something happening to his child and took all the necessary precautions. Jasmine learnt to relieve herself in a bucket that he cleans every day and also to wait for him. She's able to move freely within the four walls adapted so that nothing happens to her.

It's been a long time since he felt that this house was his home. It was a space in which to sleep and eat. A place of broken words and silences encapsulated between walls, of accumulated sadnesses that splintered the air, scraped away at it, split open the particles of oxygen. A house where madness was brewing, where it lurked, imminent.

But ever since Jasmine arrived, the house has been full of her wild smell and her bright and silent laughter.

He goes into the room that was once Leo's. He's taken down the wallpaper with boats on it and painted the room white. There's also a new cot and furniture. Buying these things wasn't an option so he built them by hand. He didn't want to arouse suspicion. After his day at the plant, he likes to get down on the floor and imagine what colour he's going to paint the cot. He wants to decide the moment the baby is born. When he looks his child in the eye, he imagines he'll know what colour to choose. For the first few months, the baby will sleep by his side, next to his bed, in a temporary cot.

That way he can make sure this child doesn't stop breathing.

Jasmine always sits with him in the baby's room. He prefers it this way, for her to follow him around. All of the drawers in the house have locks on them. One day when he got home from the plant, Jasmine had taken out all the knives. She'd cut one of her hands. She was sitting on the floor, covered in the blood that was slowly dripping from her. He panicked. But it was only a superficial wound. He treated it, cleaned her up and locked away the knives. And the forks and spoons. When he cleaned the floor, he discovered that she'd been trying to draw on the wood. That's when he bought her the crayons and paper.

He also bought cameras that connect to his phone so that while he's at the plant, he can see what Jasmine is doing in the room. She spends hours watching television, sleeping, drawing, staring at a fixed point. At times, it seems she's thinking, like she really can.

4

"Have you ever eaten something that's alive?"

"I haven't."

"There's a vibration, a subtle and fragile heat, that makes a living being particularly delicious. You're extracting life by the mouthful. It's the pleasure of knowing that because of your intent, your actions, this being has ceased to exist. It's the feeling of a complex and precious organism expiring little by little, and also becoming part of you. For always. I find this miracle fascinating. This possibility of an indissoluble union."

Urlet is drinking wine from a glass that looks like an antique chalice. It's a transparent red, made of etched crystal, and has strange figures on it. The figures could be naked women dancing around a bonfire. Or not. They're abstract. Perhaps men howling. Urlet picks the glass up by the stem and raises it very slowly, as though it were an object of extraordinary value. The cup is the same colour as the band he wears around his ring finger.

He looks at Urlet's nails, he always does, and can't help but feel disgust. The man's nails are neat but long. There's something hypnotic and primitive about them. There's something of a wail, of an ancient presence to them. Something about Urlet's nails creates a need to feel the touch of his fingers.

It occurs to him that he only has to see the man a few times a year and he's glad.

Urlet is sitting against the tall back of an armchair made of dark wood. Behind him hang half a dozen human heads. His hunting trophies. He always clarifies, to whoever will listen, that over the years these were the toughest heads to hunt, those that posed "monstrous and invigorating challenges". Next to the heads hang framed antique photographs. They're classic photographs of black people being hunted in Africa before the Transition. The largest and sharpest image shows a white hunter down on his knees holding a rifle, and behind him, on stakes, the heads of four black men. The hunter is smiling.

He finds it difficult to determine Urlet's age. The man is one of those people who seems to have been part of the world since the beginning, but who have a certain vitality, and as a result appear young. Forty, fifty, Urlet could be seventy. Impossible to know.

Urlet remains silent and looks at him.

He thinks that Urlet collects words in addition to trophies. They're worth as much to the man as a head hanging on the wall. His Spanish is near perfect and he expresses himself in a precious manner. Urlet selects each word as though the wind would carry it away if he didn't, as though his sentences could be vitrified in the air, and he could take hold of them and lock them away with a key in some piece of furniture, but not just any piece, an antique, an art nouveau piece with glass doors.

Urlet left Romania after the Transition. The hunting of humans was prohibited there and he'd owned a game reserve for animals. He wanted to stay in the business and decided to move elsewhere.

He never knows what to say to Urlet. The man looks at him as though in expectation of some revelatory sentence or lucid word, but he just wants to leave. He says the first thing that comes to mind nervously, because he can't hold Urlet's gaze, nor can he stop the feeling that inside this man there's a presence, something clawing at his body, trying to get out.

"Sure, it must be fascinating to eat something that's alive."

Urlet makes a slight movement with his mouth. It's a gesture of contempt. He sees this clearly and recognizes it as such because on every visit, at some point during their conversation, Urlet finds a way to make his displeasure known. Displeasure at this man who repeats his words or who has nothing new to add or whose responses don't allow for further elaboration. But Urlet's gestures are measured and he takes care to ensure they go almost unnoticed. He smiles right away and says, "Indeed, my dear *cavaler*."

Urlet never uses his name and always addresses him with formality. He calls him *cavaler*, Romanian for gentleman.

It's daytime, but in Urlet's office, behind the imposing desk of black wood, behind the chair that looks like a throne, below the stuffed heads and photographs, are lit candles. As though the space were a great altar, as though the heads were holy objects from some private religion, Urlet's religion, dedicated to the collection of humans, words, photographs, flavours, souls, meats, books, presences.

The walls of the office are lined with floor-to-ceiling shelves filled with old books. Most of the titles are in

Romanian, and though he's at a distance he can make out a few: *Necronomicon, The Book of Saint Cyprian, Enchiridion of Pope Leo, The Grand Grimoire, Book of the Dead.*

They hear the laughter of the hunters returning from the game reserve.

Urlet gives him the paperwork for the next order. He can't help but shudder when one of the man's fingernails grazes his hand. He pulls it away quickly, unable to hide his disgust, unwilling to look Urlet in the eye, because he's afraid that the presence, the entity that lives under the man's skin, will cease clawing at him and be set free. Is it the soul of a being Urlet ate alive, one that got trapped inside him, he wonders.

He looks at the order and sees the red circle Urlet has drawn around "impregnated females".

"I don't want any more females that haven't been impregnated. They're idiotic and submissive."

"That's fine. Impregnated females cost three times as much. From four months on, the cost goes up further."

"Not a problem. I want a few with the fetus developed, so it can be eaten afterwards."

"That's fine. I see you've increased the number of males."

"The males you deliver are the best on the market. They're increasingly agile and intelligent, as if that were possible."

An assistant knocks softly on the door. Urlet tells him to come in. The assistant goes up to Urlet and whispers something in his ear. Urlet gestures to the man, who leaves in silence, closing the door behind him.

Still seated, uncomfortable, unsure what to do, he sees the assistant leave and the smile that forms on Urlet's face.

Urlet taps the table with his nails slowly. He doesn't stop grinning.

"My dear *cavaler*, fate has smiled down upon me. Some time ago, I implemented a programme that allows celebrities who have fallen from grace by amassing large debts to settle their accounts here."

"What do you mean? I don't follow."

Urlet takes another sip of wine. He waits a few seconds before answering.

"They are required to remain on the game reserve for one week, three days or a few hours, depending on the amount they owe, and if the hunters aren't able to get them, and they survive the adventure, I guarantee the cancellation of all of their debt."

"So they're willing to die because they owe money?"

"There are people willing to do atrocious things for a lot less, *cavaler*. Like hunting someone who's famous and eating them."

Urlet's answer perplexes him. He never would have thought the man capable of judging someone for eating a person. "Does this pose a moral dilemma for you? Do you find it atrocious?" he asks.

"Not at all. The human being is complex and I find the vile acts, contradictions and sublimities characteristic of our condition astonishing. Our existence would be an exasperating shade of grey if we were all flawless."

"But then why do you consider it atrocious?"

"Because it is. But that's what's incredible, that we accept our excesses, that we naturalize them, that we embrace our primitive essence."

Urlet pauses to pour more wine and offers him some. He doesn't accept, says he has to drive. Urlet resumes, speaking slowly. He touches the band around his ring finger, moves it. "After all, since the world began, we've been eating each other. If not symbolically, then we've been literally gorging on each other. The Transition has enabled us to be less hypocritical."

Urlet gets up slowly and says, "Follow me, *cavaler*. Let us take pleasure in the atrocity."

He thinks that the only thing he wants to do is go home and be with Jasmine and put his hand on her belly. But there's something about Urlet that's magnetic and repulsive. He gets up and follows him.

They walk over to a large window that opens onto the game reserve. In the stone courtyard, half a dozen hunters are taking pictures with their trophies. Some of them are kneeling down on the ground, over the bodies of their prey. Two of the hunters have grabbed hold of their preys' hair, and are displaying the raised heads. One has shot an impregnated female. He figures she's about six months.

In the centre of the group, one hunter has his prey upright. The male is propped against the hunter's body and an assistant is supporting him from behind. He's the best catch, the one worth the most. The male's clothes are dirty, but they're clearly expensive, good quality. He recognizes the male as a musician, as the rock star who's gone into debt. But he can't remember his name, just knows he was very famous.

The assistants go up to the hunters and ask for their rifles. The hunters drape their prey over their shoulders and go to a barn where each is weighed, labelled and delivered to the chefs, who will cut them up and separate the pieces they'll cook from those that will be vacuum sealed for the hunters to take with them.

The game reserve offers hunters a packaging service for their heads.

5

Urlet sees him out, but at the entrance to the parlour they run into a hunter who arrived after the others. It's Guerrero Iraola, a man he knows well. Guerrero Iraola used to provide the plant with heads. His is one of the largest breeding centres, but over time he began sending Krieg sick and violent heads, he'd be late with orders, and inject the product with experimental drugs to tenderize the meat. He hasn't ordered heads from the breeding centre since then because ultimately, the meat was low grade and he grew tired of the dismissive way things were handled, of never being able to speak to Guerrero Iraola directly, of having to go through three secretaries to talk to the man for less than five minutes.

"Marcos Tejo! How are you doing, mate? It's been forever."

"I'm doing well, very well."

"Urlet, this gentleman is sitting down for a meal with us. No discussion," Guerrero Iraola says, in a mix of Spanish and stilted English.

"As you wish," Urlet says and nods slightly. Then he gestures to one of the assistants and says something in his ear.

"Join us for lunch, the hunt was pretty spectacular," Guerrero Iraola says, switching to English again. "We all want to try Ulises Vox."

Right, that's the name of the rock star who had gone into debt, he thinks. The possibility of eating the man seems aberrant to him, and he says, "I have a long trip home."

"No discussion," Guerrero Iraola repeats in English. "For old times' sake, since I hope they'll return."

He knows that being taken off the list of providers didn't make much of a difference to the man, at least not economically. After all, the Guerrero Iraola Breeding Centre provides half the country with heads and exports a huge volume of product. But he also knows that the centre took a hit in terms of prestige because the Krieg Processing Plant is the most reputable in the business. But there's a rule that's never broken: stay on good terms with the providers, even this one who exasperates him with the mix of Spanish and English he uses to show his roots, so that everyone knows he went to private bilingual schools, and that he comes from a long line of breeders, first of animals and now of humans. One never knows if they'll have to do business with someone like him again.

Urlet doesn't give him a chance to answer and says, "Of course, the *cavaler* will be delighted to join us. My assistants are adding a plate to the table."

"Great," Guerrero Iraola says in English, then continues in Spanish. "And I imagine that you, sir, will be joining us as well?"

"It will be an honour," Urlet says.

They step into the parlour where the hunters are seated in the high-backed leather armchairs, smoking cigars. They've already taken off their boots and vests, and the assistants have given them jackets and ties for lunch.

An assistant rings a bell and they all get up and move to the dining room where a table has been set with dinnerware from England, silver knives, crystal glasses. The napkins are embroidered with the game reserve's initials. The chairs have high backs with seats of red velvet, and the candelabra have been lit.

Before he enters the dining room, he's asked to follow an assistant. The man hands him a jacket to try on and a matching tie. He thinks that all the preparations are ridiculous, but he has to respect Urlet's rules.

When he enters the dining room, the other hunters look at him with surprise, as though he were an intruder. But Guerrero Iraola introduces him. "This is Marcos Tejo, the right-hand man at the Krieg Processing Plant. This guy's one of the most knowledgeable in the business," Guerrero Iraola says, switching to English again. "He's the most respected and most demanding."

He'd never introduce himself this way to anyone. If he had to honestly tell others who he was, he'd say: "This is Marcos Tejo, a man whose son died and who moves through life with a hole in his chest. A man who's married to a broken woman. This man slaughters humans because he needs to support his father, who's lost his mind, is locked up in a nursing home and doesn't recognize him. He's going to have a child with a female, one of the most serious crimes a person can commit, but he doesn't care in the slightest, and the child is going to be his."

The hunters greet him and Guerrero Iraola tells him to take a seat by his side.

He needs to be on his way home. The trip is going to take several hours. But he glances at his phone and sees that Jasmine is sleeping, and relaxes.

The assistants serve fennel and anise soup followed by a starter of fingers in a sherry reduction with candied vegetables. But they don't use the Spanish word for fingers. They say "fresh fingers", in English, as if doing so could resignify the fact that what's being served are the fingers of several humans who were breathing a few hours ago.

Guerrero Iraola is talking about the Lulú cabaret. He's using code words because it's known that the place is a seedy club involved in human trafficking, with one minor difference: after paying for sex, a client can also pay to eat the woman he's slept with. It's extremely pricey but the option exists, even if it's illegal. Everyone is involved: politicians, the police, judges. Each takes their cut because human trafficking has gone from being the third largest industry to the first. Only a few of the women are eaten, but from time to time it happens, that's what Guerrero Iraola is telling them, emphasizing in English that he paid "billions, billions" for a stunning blonde who drove him wild and afterwards, he of course, "had to take things further". The hunters laugh and clink their glasses, celebrating his decision.

"So how was she?" one of the youngest hunters asks him.

Guerrero Iraola can only raise his fingers to his mouth in a gesture indicating that she was tasty. No one can admit in public that they've eaten a person with a first and last name, except in the case of the musician who gave his consent. But Guerrero Iraola hints at it to show Krieg's right-hand man he's got the money to pay for it. That's why Guerrero Iraola invited him to lunch, to rub his face in it. He hears one of the hunters, who's sitting close by, whisper to another that the stunning blonde was in fact a young virgin of fourteen who needed to be tenderized and that Guerrero Iraola destroyed her in bed, raping her for hours. The man says he was there and that the child was half-dead when they took her away to be slaughtered.

It occurs to him that in this case, the flesh trade is literal, and he's disgusted. While he thinks about this, he tries to eat the candied vegetables, avoiding the fingers that have been cut into small pieces.

He's sitting next to Urlet, and the man looks at him, and says into his ear, "You have to respect what's being served, *cavaler.* Every dish contains death. Think of it as a sacrifice that some have made for others."

Urlet's nails graze his hand again and he shudders. He thinks he can hear the scratching under the man's skin, the contained wail, the presence that wants to get out. He swallows the "fresh fingers" because he wants this to be over with, to leave as quickly as possible. Urlet's false theories are not something he cares to argue about. He's not going to tell the man that a sacrifice generally requires consent from the person being sacrificed, nor will he comment that everything contains death, not just this dish, and that he, Urlet, is also dying with every second that passes, like all of them.

To his surprise, the fingers are exquisite. He realizes how much he misses eating meat.

An assistant brings out a single plate and serves it to the hunter who killed the musician. Solemnly the assistant says, "The tongue of Ulises Vox marinated in fine herbs, served over kimchi and lemon-dressed potatoes."

They all applaud and laugh. Someone says, "It's a privilege to eat Ulises's tongue. You'll have to sing one of his songs afterwards so we can see if you sound like him."

They all burst into laughter. Except for him. He doesn't laugh.

The rest of the diners are served the heart, eyes, kidneys and buttocks. Ulises Vox's penis is placed in front of Guerrero Iraola, who requested it.

"Looks like he had a big one," Guerrero Iraola says.

"What, are you a fag now, eating a dick," one of them says to him.

They all laugh.

"No, it makes me more potent sexually. It's an aphrodisiac," Guerrero Iraola answers seriously, and looks at the man who called him a fag with contempt.

They all go quiet. No one wants to contradict him because he's a man with a lot of power. To change the subject and release the tension, someone asks, "What's this we're eating, this kimchi?"

There's silence. No one knows what kimchi is, not even Guerrero Iraola, a man who's had some education, who's travelled the world, who speaks different languages. Urlet does a very good job of hiding his displeasure at dining with the uncultured, unrefined people that surround him. But he doesn't hide it completely. There's a hint of disdain in his voice when he answers. "Kimchi is a food prepared with vegetables that have been fermented for one month. It's Korean in origin. The benefits are numerous, among them that it's a probiotic. Nothing but the best for my guests."

"We're getting probiotics from all the hard drugs Ulises injected," one of them says and they all laugh loudly.

Urlet doesn't respond, just regards them with a half-smile stuck on his face. He looks at Urlet and knows that the entity, whatever it is that's in there, scratching at the man's skin from the inside, wants to howl and slice through the air with a sharp, cutting wail.

Guerrero Iraola gives them a look that restores order, and asks a question: "How was Ulises Vox hunted?"

"I caught him off guard in what appeared to be a hiding spot. He had the bad luck of moving just as I walked by," the hunter says.

"Right, with your bionic ear, no one gets away," says the man who shot the pregnant female.

"Lisandrito is a master," Guerrero Iraola says, the last word in English, "like all of the Núñez Guevaras. The family's got the best hunters in the country." He points his fork full of flesh to the hunter and says, "Next time Urlet has a celebrity for us, leave him for me, kid." It's a clear threat and Lisandrito lowers his eyes.

Guerrero Iraola raises his glass and they all toast Lisandrito and his lineage of first-class hunters.

"How many days did he have left?" someone asks Urlet.

"Today was his last day. He had five hours left."

They all applaud and clink their glasses.

Except for him. He's thinking of Jasmine.

6

He knows he'll be home late. It's a long drive, but he doesn't want to stay in a hotel like he used to, before Jasmine. He's been on the road for several hours and knows it'll be night when he gets in.

He passes the abandoned zoo but doesn't stop because it's dark and because he never wants to return. The last time he was there he didn't yet know that Jasmine was pregnant. He needed to clear his mind and wanted to go to the aviary.

As he neared the building, he heard shouts and laughter. The sounds were coming from the serpentarium. He approached slowly, rounding the aviary to see if he could find a window so he wouldn't have to go inside.

One of the walls was broken. He went up to it cautiously and saw a group of teenagers. There were six or seven of them. They were holding sticks.

The teenagers were in the puppies' serpentarium. They'd broken the glass. He could see that the puppies were in there, curled up against each other, trembling, whimpering with fear.

Weeks before, he'd petted those puppies. Now he saw a teenager grab one of the four brothers and throw him into the air. Another teenager, the tallest of the lot, hit the pup with a stick, as though he were a ball. The creature struck the wall and fell to the floor, dead, very close to one of his brothers, who had already been killed.

They all applauded and one of them said, "Let's smash their brains against the wall. I wanna see what it feels like."

He grabbed the third puppy and struck the animal's head repeatedly against the wall. "It's like smashing a melon or a piece of shit. Let's see what happens with the last one."

The last puppy tried to defend himself, to bark. That's Jagger, he thought, while his rage ate away at him because he knew he couldn't save the pup, because he wouldn't be able to stop them on his own. Jagger bit the hand of the teenager who was about to throw him into the air. As he looked on at the scene, he felt a sense of pleasure at Jagger's small revenge.

The teenagers laughed, at first, but then they grew still, silent.

"You're gonna die, idiot. I told you to grab it by the neck."

The teenager was quiet, he didn't know how to react.

"Now you have the virus."

"You're contaminated."

"You're gonna die."

The others all took a few steps back, in fear.

"The virus is a lie, dickheads."

"But the government..."

"What about the government? You don't actually believe that lot of corrupt leeches, the fucking motherfuckers we have for a government."

While the teenager was saying this, he shook Jagger in the air.

"No, but there were people who died."

"Don't be an idiot. Can't you see they're controlling us? If we eat each other, they control overpopulation, poverty, crime. Do you want me to keep going? I mean it's obvious."

"Yeah, like in that movie that was banned where at the end everyone's eating each other and they don't know it," the tallest one said.

"What movie?"

"The movie was... it was called *Destiny is Catching Up to Us* or something dumb like that. We saw it on the dark web, it's hard to find because it's banned."

"Oh yeah, mate, I remember it. It's the one where they eat those green crackers that are really made of people."

The teenager holding Jagger continued to shake the puppy in the air, with more force, and shouted, "I'm not gonna die for this piece of shit of an animal."

He said it with resentment and fear, and threw Jagger hard against the wall. Jagger fell to the floor, but was still alive, crying, whining.

"What if we light it on fire?" another one asked.

And he could take no more.

7

Every so often, an inspector from the Office of the Undersecretary for the Control of Domestic Heads shows up at his house. He knows all the inspectors, all those who matter, because when they shut down the Faculty of Veterinary Sciences, when the world was in chaos, when his father began to want to live inside books and would call at three in the morning asking to speak with the Baron in the Trees, so that the man could help him get into the pages, when his father later told him that books were spies from a parallel dimension, when animals became a threat, when at a chilling speed the world was put back together and cannibalism legitimized, he worked there, at the undersecretary's office. They'd recruited him based on the recommendation of employees from his father's processing plant. He was one of the people who drafted the regulations and rules, but he lasted less than a year because the salary was low and he had to put his father in the nursing home.

The office first began sending inspectors a few days after the female was brought to his house. The female who at the time had no name, who was a number in a registry, a problem, one domestic head like so many others.

The inspector was young and didn't know he'd worked for the undersecretary. He took the man to the barn where the female was lying on a blanket, tied up, naked. The inspector didn't seem surprised and only asked if she'd been given the required vaccines.

"She was a gift and I'm still getting used to her being here. But she's been vaccinated, I'll get the papers for you."

"You could always sell her. She's an FGP, she's worth a fortune. I have a list of interested buyers."

"I'm not sure what I'm going to do yet."

"I don't see anything out of the ordinary. My only suggestion is to clean her up a little to prevent disease. Remember that if you decide to slaughter her, you'll need to contact a specialist who'll verify you've done so and notify us for our records. The same goes for selling her, or if she escapes, or if anything else happens that should be recorded, so we don't have any issues down the road."

"Okay, everything's clear. If I want to slaughter her, I'm certified to do so. I work at a processing plant. How's El Gordo Pineda doing?"

"You mean Señor Alfonso Pineda?"

"Yeah, El Gordo."

"No one calls him that, he's not fat, and he's our boss."

"So El Gordo's a boss. That I can't believe. I worked with him back when we were kids. Send him my regards."

After that first visit, El Gordo Pineda himself called to say that the next time an inspector stopped by, they'd only ask for his signature, so as not to bother him.

"Hi, Tejito. Imagine you of all people with a female."

"Gordo, it's been ages, mate."

"Hey, I'm not fat any more! The wife's got me drinking juice and other crap that healthy people eat. Now I'm thin and miserable. When are we gonna have ourselves a barbecue, Tejito?"

El Gordo Pineda had been his partner back when they'd started carrying out inspections of the first domestic heads. The owners knew what was prohibited and what wasn't, but they didn't expect visits from inspectors and the two of them witnessed all sorts of things.

The regulations were adapted on the job. He remembers one case where a woman answered the door. They asked the woman about the female in the home and needed to see her papers, verify that she'd been vaccinated and take a look at her living conditions. The woman got nervous and said that her husband, the female's owner, wasn't home, and that they'd have to come back later. He looked at El Gordo and the two of them had the same thought. They moved the woman aside as she was trying to close the door and entered the house. She shouted that they weren't allowed to come in, that it was illegal and she was going to call the police. El Gordo told her that they were authorized to do so and said she could call the police if she wanted to. They went from room to room but the female wasn't there. Then it occurred to him to open closets, check under beds. Eventually they looked in the couple's room. Underneath the bed was a wooden box with small wheels that was big enough to hold a person lying down. When they opened it, they saw the female, in what looked like a coffin, unable to move. They didn't know what to do because regulations hadn't been drafted for a case of this nature. The female was healthy and though the wooden coffin wasn't a conventional place to keep her, it wasn't reason enough to fine the owner. When the woman walked into the room and saw they'd discovered the female, she broke down. She began to cry and told them that her husband had sex with the head and not with her, that she couldn't take it any more, she'd been replaced by an animal, and couldn't bear the idea of sleeping with that disgusting creature under the bed. She was humiliated and if they sent her to the Municipal Slaughterhouse for being an accomplice, she didn't care, all she wanted was to go back to a normal life, to life before the Transition. With that statement, they were able to call the team in charge of examining heads for evidence that they'd been "enjoyed", which was the official word used in such cases. The regulations specify that reproduction is only permitted by artificial means. Semen must be purchased in special banks, and sample implantation carried out by qualified professionals. The whole process has to be documented and certified so that if the female is impregnated, the fetus already has an identification number. As such, domestic females should be virgins. Having sex with a head, enjoying her, is illegal and the sentence is death in the Municipal Slaughterhouse. The special team went to the house and confirmed that the female had been enjoyed "in every possible way". The owner, a man of around sixty, was sentenced and sent directly to the Municipal Slaughterhouse. The woman was fined and the female confiscated and sold for a low price in an auction because of what is officially referred to as "proscribed enjoyment".

He's only had a few hours of sleep after the long drive from the game reserve when he wakes with a start. A car horn is honking. Jasmine, who's at his side, looks at him, her eyes open wide. She's used to keeping still, to watching him, because she sleeps all day and at night he needs her not to move much. That's why he started tying her to the bed, and she got used to it. He doesn't want Jasmine wandering through the house when he can't keep an eye on her. He doesn't want her to get hurt or for something to happen to his child.

He jumps out of bed and moves the curtain aside. A man in a suit is standing next to a car with the door open and bending down periodically to honk the horn.

"It's an inspector," he thinks.

He opens the front door, in pyjamas, his face twisted with sleep.

"Señor Marcos Tejo?"

"That's me."

"I'm from the Office of the Undersecretary for the Control of Domestic Heads. The last inspection was almost five months ago, is that right?"

"That's correct. Show me where to sign so I can go back to sleep."

The inspector looks at him with surprise at first, and then with authority, and raising his voice, says, "Excuse me? Where's the female, Señor Tejo?"

"Look, El Gordo Pineda called to tell me that you'd only need a signature. The last inspector didn't have a problem."

"You mean Señor Pineda? He doesn't work in the department any more."

A shiver runs along his spine. He tries to think. If the inspector finds out that Jasmine is pregnant, they'll send him to the Municipal Slaughterhouse. But worse still is they'll take his child away.

He tries to buy himself some time to figure out what to do. "Why don't you come in for some *mate*, I'm half-asleep," he says. "Just give me a few minutes to wake up."

"I appreciate the offer but I have to get going. Where's the female?"

"Come on, just for a bit. You can tell me what happened to Pineda," he says, sweating, trying not to show he's nervous.

The inspector hesitates and then says, "All right, but I can't stay long."

They sit down in the kitchen. He lights the stove and puts the kettle on the burner. As he's getting the *mate* ready, he rambles on about the weather, and about how bad the roads are in the area, and asks the inspector if he likes the work. When he hands the man the *mate*, he says, "Will you give me a few minutes to wash my face? I got back from a long drive yesterday and I've had almost no sleep. You woke me up with all your honking."

"But before I honked I was clapping my hands for a while."

"Really? I apologize. I'm a deep sleeper, I didn't hear a thing."

The inspector is uncomfortable. It's clear he wants to leave, but Pineda's name drew him into the house and that's what's keeping him there.

With the inspector in the kitchen, he goes to his room and sees that Jasmine is still in bed. He closes the door and as he walks to the bathroom to wash his face, thinks: What should I do? What should I say?

He returns to the kitchen and offers the inspector some biscuits. The man accepts them with distrust.

"Did they get rid of El Gordo Pineda?"

The inspector doesn't answer right away. He tenses up. "How do you know him?" he asks.

"I used to work with him back when he were kids. We're friends, we were inspectors at the same time. We did your job when hardly any of the regulations had been finalized. we were the ones who adapted them."

The inspector seems to relax a little and looks at him with different eyes. With a degree of admiration. He helps himself to another biscuit and there's a hint of what could be a smile on his face.

"I just started, I've been doing this for less than two months. They promoted Señor Pineda. I never worked for him, but I'm told he was a great boss."

He's relieved, but hides it. "Yeah, El Gordo's something else. Just give me a second," he says, and goes to his room to get his phone. He dials El Gordo's number and returns to the kitchen.

"Gordo, how have you been? Look, I'm here with one of your inspectors. He wants me to show him the female, but the thing is I haven't slept and she's out in the barn, and I'd have to open it up—it'll be a whole ordeal. Didn't I just have to sign and that was that?"

He hands the phone to the inspector.

"Yes, sir. Of course. We hadn't been informed. Right, from now on. Consider it taken care of."

The inspector places the *mate* off to the side, searches in his briefcase and pulls out a form and a pen. He smiles in a way that's artificial, tense. It's a smile that hides several questions and one threat: What are you doing with the female? Are you enjoying her? Are we talking illegal use of another's property? Just you wait until El Gordo Pineda isn't around any more. Just you wait, you with your special privileges, you're going to pay.

He sees this clearly. The questions and the veiled threat. But he doesn't care. He knows he can fake a certificate for domestic slaughter, the plant has everything he needs. That, and he can no longer depend on El Gordo Pineda, not after this visit. He wants the inspector to leave, he wants to go back to sleep, even though he knows it won't be possible. He hands back the form and says, "Did you want more *mate*?"

The inspector gets up slowly. He puts the form in his briefcase and says, "No, thank you. I'll be on my way."

He sees the inspector to the door and holds out his hand. The man's hand doesn't grasp his; it's limp, lifeless, so that he has to make an effort to shake it, to support the hand that's like an amorphous mass, a dead fish. Before turning away, the inspector looks him in the eye and says, "This job would be pretty easy if everyone could just sign and not do anything else, don't you think?"

He doesn't say anything. What he thinks is that it's an impertinence, even if he does understand. He understands the powerlessness felt by this young inspector who needs something out of the ordinary to happen so his day will be worthwhile, this inspector who's suspicious about the whole scene and has to resign himself to not doing his job, this inspector who's clearly not corrupt, who never would have accepted a bribe, who's an honest man because there are a few things he doesn't understand yet, this inspector who reminds him so much of himself when he was young (before the processing plant, the doubts, his baby, the series of daily deaths), and thought that complying with regulations was what mattered most, when in some inaccessible corner of his mind, he was glad about the Transition, glad to have this new job, to be part of this historic change, to be thinking about the rules that people would have to comply with long after he'd disappeared from the world, because the regulations, he'd thought, "are my legacy, the mark I'll leave behind".

He never would have imagined he'd break the very law he established.

8

When he's sure the inspector has left and that the man's car is past the gate, he goes back to his room, unties Jasmine and hugs her. He hugs her tight and puts his hand on her belly.

He cries a little and Jasmine looks at him. Though she doesn't understand, she touches his face gently, and it's almost like a caress.

9

He has the day off.

He makes some sandwiches, grabs a beer and some water for Jasmine. Then he gets the old radio, the one he listened to when Koko and Pugliese were still alive, and he takes Jasmine to the tree where the dogs are buried. The two of them sit in the shade, listening to instrumental jazz.

The station plays Miles Davis, Coltrane, Charlie Parker, Dizzy Gillespie. There are no words, only the music and the sky, its blue so immense it shimmers, and the leaves of the tree barely moving, and Jasmine leaning silently against his chest.

When Thelonious Monk comes on, he stands up and slowly brings Jasmine to her feet. He holds her carefully and begins to move, to sway. At first Jasmine doesn't understand and seems uncomfortable, but then she lets go and smiles. He kisses her on the forehead, on the mark where she's been branded. They dance slowly, though it's a fast song.

They spend the rest of the afternoon beneath the tree and he thinks he can feel Koko and Pugliese dancing with them.

10

He wakes to Nélida's call.

"Hi, Marcos, how are you, dear? Your father's a tad out of sorts, nothing serious, but we need you to stop by, today if possible."

"I don't think I can make it today, tomorrow's better."

"You're not understanding me. We need you to come in today."

He doesn't answer. He knows what Nélida's call means, but doesn't want to say it, he can't put it into words.

"I'll leave now, Nélida."

First he takes Jasmine to her room. He knows it'll be a while before he's back so he leaves enough food and water for the whole day. Then he calls Mari and tells her he won't be coming in to the plant.

He speeds to the nursing home. Not because he thinks it's going to change things or because he believes he'll see his father alive, but because the speed helps stop him from thinking. He lights a cigarette and drives. But he starts to cough hard, and tosses it out the window. The cough doesn't subside. He feels something in his chest, like there's a stone in there. He thumps on it and coughs.

Then he pulls over to the side of the highway and rests his head on the steering wheel. He sits there in silence, trying to breathe. The entrance to the zoo is right next to him. He looks at the sign. It's broken and stripped of paint, and the animals drawn around the word "zoo" are almost impossible to make out. He leaves the car and walks to the entrance. The sign sits on a lintel arch made of uneven stones. The arch isn't very high up and he climbs onto the stones and stands behind the sign. He starts to kick the sign, to hit it, to move it until he's able to push it over onto the ground. The sign hits the grass with a dull sound, a thud.

Now this place has no name.

When he arrives at the nursing home, Nélida is waiting for him at the door. She gives him a hug. "Hi, dear, I don't have to say it, do I? I didn't want to tell you over the phone, but we needed you to come in today, to take care of the paperwork. I'm so sorry, Marcos, I'm so very sorry."

All he says is: "I want to see him now."

"Of course, dear, I'll take you to his room."

Nélida leads him to his father's room. There's a lot of natural light in the room and everything is in its place. On the night table sits a photo of his mother holding him in her arms when he was a baby. There are pill bottles and a lamp.

He sits down on a chair next to the bed in which his father lies. The man's hands are crossed over his chest. His hair has been combed and his body perfumed. He's dead.

"When did it happen?"

"Today, in the early hours. He died in his sleep."

Nélida closes the door and leaves him alone.

When he touches his father's hands, he finds that they're freezing and can't help but move his away. He doesn't feel anything. What he wants to do is cry and hug his father, but he looks at the body as though it were a stranger's.

Now his father is free from the madness, he thinks, from this horrific world, and he feels something like relief, but in fact the stone in his chest is getting bigger.

He goes over to the window that opens onto the garden. A hummingbird hovers right at the level of his eyes. For a few seconds, the bird seems to be watching him. He wishes he could touch it, but it moves quickly and disappears. He thinks there's no way that something so beautiful and small could cause harm. He thinks that just maybe the hummingbird is his father's spirit saying goodbye.

It's then that he feels the stone shift in his chest and the tears begin to fall.

11

He leaves the room. Nélida asks him to follow her so he can sign the papers. They step into her office and she offers him a cup of coffee, which he turns down. Nélida is nervous; she shuffles the papers, takes a sip of water. He thinks that this should be routine for her, that there's no reason to be holding up the paperwork as she is.

"What's your problem, Nélida?"

Nélida looks at him, disconcerted. He's never been this direct, or this aggressive.

"It's nothing, dear, just that I had to call your sister."

She looks at him with a bit of guilt, but also resolve.

"These are the nursing home's rules and there are no exceptions. You know I adore you, dear, but I'd be putting my job at risk. Who knows what we'd be dealing with if your sister showed up and made a scene. It wouldn't be the first time it's happened."

"That's fine."

On other occasions, he would have consoled her and said something like "Don't worry about it" or "No problem". But not today.

"You'll have to sign the consent form to cremate him. Your sister has already sent it back with a virtual signature, but she clarified that she won't be able to attend the cremation. We can make the call to the funeral parlour if you like."

"Go ahead."

"Of course, you'll have to attend the cremation, to confirm it's taken place. They'll give you the urn there."

"That's fine."

"Will you be wanting a simulacrum of a funeral?"

"No."

"Of course, almost no one has them now. But what about the farewell service?"

"No."

Nélida looks at him with surprise. She drinks some more water and crosses her arms. "Your sister would like to have the service, and legally, she has the right. I understand you're in denial, but she's determined to say goodbye."

He breathes deeply, feels a crushing exhaustion. The stone is now the size of his whole chest. He's not going to argue with anyone. Not with Nélida, not with his sister, not with all the people who will attend the simulacrum of a wake, what they call a "farewell service", just to be on good terms with his sister, even though these people never knew his father, and didn't once take it upon themselves to ask how he was. Then he laughs and says, "Fine, let her have the service. Let her take care of something for once. Just one thing."

Nélida looks at him with surprise and a bit of pity. "I understand your anger and you have reason to feel the way you do, but she's your sister. You only have one family."

He tries to recall when it was, exactly, that Nélida went from being a nursing home employee to someone who believes she has the right to give advice and her opinion, and to fall again and again into platitudes and irritating clichés.

"Give me the papers, Nélida. Please."

Nélida recoils. She looks at him, taken aback. He's always been kind to her, affectionate even. She gives him the papers in silence. He signs them and says, "I want him to be cremated today, now."

"Okay, dear. After the Transition, everything was sped up. Take a seat in the waiting room and I'll look after it. They'll come get him in a regular car, just so you know. Hearses are no longer used."

"Yeah, everyone knows that."

"Right, well, I just wanted to clarify it because there are a lot of clueless people who think that things haven't changed when it comes to these matters."

"How could things not have changed after the attacks? It was in all the papers. No one wants their dead family member to be eaten en route to the cemetery, Nélida."

"I'm sorry, it's just that I'm nervous, and I'm not thinking clearly. I cared a lot about your father and all of this is very difficult for me."

There's a long silence. He's unwilling to concede an apology in return. Instead, he looks at her impatiently and she gets upset.

"I know it's not for me to ask, Marcos, but are you okay? This is very sad news, I know that, but for some time now you've been a bit off, you have bags under your eyes, you seem tired."

He looks at her without saying anything and she continues, "All right, well what's going to happen is that you'll go there in the car and you'll be next to your father at all times, including during the cremation."

"I know, Nélida. I've been through this before."

She goes white. Of course, it hadn't occurred to her, not until now. Nélida gets up quickly and says, "I'm sorry, I'm an old fool. I'm sorry." She keeps apologizing until they reach the waiting room, where he sits down and she offers him something to drink before leaving in silence.

12

He drives home with his father's ashes in the car. They're on the passenger seat because he didn't know where to put the urn. The cremation was over with quickly. He saw his father's body slowly enter the oven in the transparent coffin. He didn't feel anything, or perhaps what he felt was relief.

His sister has already called four times, though he hasn't answered. He knows she's capable of driving to his house to get the ashes, he knows she's capable of anything to stick to the social convention of a farewell service for their father. Eventually he'll have to answer.

It's late when he drives past what was once the zoo, what no longer has a name. But he pulls over. There's still a bit of light.

He leaves the car with the urn in his hands. The sign is on the ground and he walks past it.

He goes straight to the aviary without even thinking about the lion's den. In the distance, he hears shouts. It must be the teenagers, he thinks, the ones who killed the puppies.

When he reaches the aviary, he climbs the stairs to the hanging bridge. He lies down and looks up at the glass roof, the orange and pink sky, the night that's approaching.

He remembers when his father brought him to the aviary. They sat right next to each other on one of the benches that used to be below the bridge, and for hours, his father told him about the different species of birds, their habits, the colours of the females and males, about birds that sang during the day or at night, about those that migrated. His father's voice was like brightly coloured candyfloss, soft, immense, beautiful. He'd never heard his father sound like this, not since the death of his mother. And when they climbed the bridge, his father pointed to the stained-glass man with wings and the birds alongside him and smiled. "Everyone says that he fell because he flew too close to the sun," his father said, "but he flew, do you see what I mean, Son? He was able to fly. It doesn't matter if you fall, if you were a bird for even just a few seconds."

For a while, he lies there, whistling a song his father used to sing: Gershwin's "Summertime". His father would always put on Ella Fitzgerald and Louis Armstrong's version. He'd say, "This is the best recording, it's the one that moves me to tears." One day he saw his parents dancing to the rhythm of Armstrong's trumpet. They moved in the half-light and he stood there for a long time, watching them in silence. His father stroked his mother's cheek and, still a young child, he felt that this was love. He couldn't put it into words, not at the time, but he knew it in his body, in the way one feels that something is true.

It was his mother who tried to teach him to whistle, though at first he couldn't get it. Then one day his father took him for a walk and showed him how it was done. "The next time your mother wants to teach you," his father said, "pretend to struggle a bit first." When he eventually did whistle in front of her, she jumped for joy, and applauded. He remembers that from that day on, the three of them would whistle together, like a sloppy trio who enjoyed themselves nonetheless. His sister, who was a baby, looked at them with bright eyes, and smiled.

He stands up, takes the lid off the urn and throws the ashes down from the bridge. They fall slowly to the ground and he says, "Bye, Dad, I'm gonna miss you."

Then he takes the stairs back down and leaves the aviary. When he reaches the playground, he crouches to gather some sand, enough to fill the urn. It's sand mixed with rubbish, but he doesn't bother to pick it out.

He sits on one of the swings and lights a cigarette. When he's done smoking, he stubs it out inside the urn and puts the lid back on.

This is what his sister's going to get: an urn full of dirty sand from an abandoned zoo with no name.

13

He drives home with the urn in the boot. His sister has now called numerous times. She calls again. He looks at his phone with impatience and puts the speaker on.

"Hi, Marquitos. Why can't I see you?"

"I'm driving."

"Oh, right. How are you doing about Dad?"

"Fine."

"I was calling to tell you that I'm planning to have the farewell service at home. It seems like the most practical option."

He doesn't say anything. The stone in his chest moves, grows.

"I wanted to ask you to bring me the urn today or tomorrow. I can also stop by your house to pick it up, though that's not ideal because of the distance, as you can imagine."

"No."

"What do you mean no?"

"No. Not today, not tomorrow. When I say so."

"But, Marqui—"

"But nothing. I'll bring you the urn when I want to and you'll have the farewell service when it's good for me. Is that clear?"

"Look, I understand that you're having a hard time, but you could talk to me in another to—"

He hangs up.

14

It's late when he gets home and he's tired. Jasmine is asleep. He knows because he's been monitoring her all day on his phone.

He doesn't open the door to her room.

Instead, he goes to the kitchen and gets a bottle of whisky. He lies down in the hammock and takes a swig. There are no stars in the sky. The night is pitch black. He doesn't see any fireflies either. It's as if the whole world has been turned off and gone silent.

He wakes with the sun, its light hitting him in the face. Off to the side, he sees the empty bottle lying on the ground. It's only when he moves and the hammock swings a little that he understands where he is.

He stumbles out of the hammock and sits down in the grass, the morning sun on his body. His head throbs between his hands. He lies on his back and looks up at the sky. It's an incandescent blue. There are no clouds and he feels that if he stretches out his arms, he'll be able to touch the blue, it seems so close.

His dream is still with him, he remembers it perfectly, but he doesn't want to think, only to lose himself in the radiant blue.

Then he lowers his arms, closes his eyes and lets the images and feelings of the dream project in his mind like a movie.

He's in the aviary. It's before the Transition, he knows because nothing has been broken yet. He's standing on the hanging bridge but there's no glass above to protect him. He looks up at the roof and sees the image of the man flying in the stained glass. The man looks at him and he lowers his eyes, not because he's surprised that the image is alive, but because he hears the deafening sound of millions of wings flapping. Only there are no birds. The aviary is empty. He looks at the man again, at Icarus, who's no longer in the stained glass. Icarus has fallen, he thinks, he's come crashing down, but he's flown. Then he looks around, and in the air on both sides of the bridge, he sees hummingbirds, ravens, robins, goldfinches, eagles, blackbirds, nightingales, bats. There are also butterflies. But they're all static. It's as though they were vitrified, like Urlet's words. As though they were inside a block of transparent amber. He feels the air becoming lighter, but the birds don't move. They all watch him, their wings open. The birds are very close, but he sees them in the distance, occupying all the space, all the air he breathes. He goes up to a hummingbird and touches it. The bird falls to the floor and shatters as though it were made of crystal. He goes up to a butterfly, its wings a light, almost phosphorescent blue. The wings tremble, vibrate, but the butterfly is still. He picks it up with both his hands, takes great care not to cause it harm. The butterfly turns to dust. He goes up to a nightingale, is about to touch it, but doesn't, his finger hovering right next to the bird because he thinks it's just beautiful and doesn't want to destroy it. The nightingale moves, flaps its wings a little and opens its beak. It doesn't sing, but lets out a cry. Its cries become piercing and desperate. They're full of hatred. He takes off, runs, flees. He leaves the aviary and finds the zoo in darkness. But he can make out the shapes of men. He realizes that the men are him, repeated infinitely. All of them have their mouths open and are naked. Though he knows they're saying something, the silence is complete. He goes up to one of the men and shakes him. He needs the man to speak, to move. The man—himself—walks so slowly it's exasperating. As he does, he goes about killing the rest of them. He doesn't hit them with a club, or strangle them, or stab them. The only thing he does is speak to them, and one by one, each man—himself—falls to the ground. Then one man—himself—comes over and hugs him. This man hugs him so tightly that he can't breathe and he struggles until he breaks free. But the man—himself—tries again, and comes over to say something into his ear. He runs away because he doesn't want to die. While he's running, he feels the stone in his chest roll around and it strikes his heart. The zoo becomes a forest. Hanging from the trees are eyes, hands, human ears and babies. He climbs one of the trees to get a baby, but when he reaches it and has it in his arms, the baby disappears. He climbs another tree and that baby turns into black smoke. He climbs another tree and the ears stick to his body. When he tries to pick them off, as though they were leeches, they rip up his skin. When he reaches the baby, he sees it's covered in human ears and is no longer breathing. Then he roars, howls, croaks, bellows, barks, meows, crows, whinnies, brays, caws, moos, cries.

When he opens his eyes, all he sees is the dazzling blue. It's then that he really does scream.

15

He needs to get going. But first he brings Jasmine food and water. As soon as he opens the door, she gives him a big hug. It's been a while since he left her alone for so many hours. He gives her a quick kiss, sits her down on the mattresses carefully and locks the door.

Today he has to go the Valka Laboratory. But before he starts the car, he dials Krieg's number.

"Hi, Marcos. Mari told me. I'm very sorry."

"Thank you."

"You don't have to go to the laboratory. I can tell them you'll stop by at a later date."

"I'll go, but it's the last time."

There's a heavy silence on Krieg's end. He's not used to being talked to in this tone of voice.

"That's not an option. I need you to go."

"I'll go today. But then I'm going to train someone else to do it."

"You're not understanding me. The laboratory is one of our highest-paying clients, I need to send the best."

"I understand you perfectly. I'm not going any more."

For a few seconds, Krieg says nothing. "All right, maybe now is not the best time to talk about this, given the circumstances."

"This is the time to talk about this and I'm not going again, or tomorrow I resign."

"What did you say? Absolutely not, Marcos. You can train someone else whenever you like. Consider the matter closed. Take as long as you need off to rest. We'll talk again later."

He hangs up without saying goodbye. He detests Doctor Valka and her laboratory of horrors.

To enter the laboratory he has to hand over his ID, undergo a retinal scan, sign several forms and be examined in a special room to ensure he has no cameras or anything else on him that could compromise the confidentiality of the experiments carried out on the premises.

A security guard takes him to the floor where the doctor is waiting for him. It's not her job to speak to processing-plant employees to ensure they bring her the best specimens, but Doctor Valka is obsessive, and a perfectionist, and as she always tells him, "The specimens are everything, I need precision if I'm going to be successful." She requires them to be FGP, the most difficult to obtain. If they're modified, she has no scruples about discarding them. She places ridiculous orders, requesting extremities with precise measures—eyes close together or far apart, a sloping forehead, a large orbital capacity, specimens that heal quickly or slowly, have large or small ears—and the list of unimaginable requests changes every time he goes to the laboratory. If a specimen doesn't meet Doctor Valka's requirements, she returns it and requests a general discount for having wasted her time and money. Of course he no longer makes mistakes.

They inevitably greet each other coolly. He holds out his hand, but without fail, she looks at him as though she doesn't understand and moves her head in a way that could be a greeting.

"How are you, Doctor Valka?"

"I've just been awarded one of the most prestigious prizes for research and innovation. As such, I'm very well."

He looks at her without answering. His only thought is that this is the last time he's going to see her, the last time he's going to hear her voice, the last time he's going to set foot in this place.

Since he doesn't congratulate her, and she's waiting for his congratulations, she says, "What was that?"

"I didn't say anything."

She looks at him, disconcerted. There was a time when he would have congratulated her.

"The work we do here at the Valka Laboratory is of vital importance, as it's through experimentation with these specimens that we're able to obtain good results. We've made significant advances that would never have been possible with animals. Our approach to specimen handling is unique and advanced, and our work protocols are strictly followed."

She keeps talking, as she always does, giving him the same marketing team speech, using words that flow like lava from a volcano that doesn't stop erupting, only it's lava that's cold and viscous. They're words that stick to one's body and all he feels is repulsion.

"What was that?" the doctor says. At some point during her monologue, she was expecting a response. She never got it because he'd stopped listening.

"I didn't say anything."

Doctor Valka looks at him with surprise. He's always been attentive, always listened to her and said what needed to be said, no more, no less, so that she felt he was interested. Doctor Valka never asks him how he's doing or if everything is okay, because she only sees him as a reflection of herself, a mirror into which she can keep talking about her achievements.

She stands up. Now is when she takes him on a tour of the laboratory, like she always does. The first few times he heaved, got stomach aches, had nightmares. The tour is useless because all he needs is the list with her order and for her to explain the requests that are most difficult to obtain. But she likes him to understand precisely what each experiment entails so that he can acquire the most suitable specimens.

Doctor Valka grabs her cane and starts off. A few years back, she had an accident with a specimen. What is known is that the accident occurred after a careless assistant left the door to a cage ajar. When the doctor, who works late into the night, did a final run through the laboratory, the specimen attacked her and bit off part of her leg. He's of the opinion that it wasn't an act of carelessness on the assistant's part, but of revenge, because Valka is notorious for being demanding and mistreating her employees, and for her cutting comments. But her laboratory is the largest and most prestigious of its kind, so people put up with her, until one day they don't. He knows that at first they called her "Doctor Mengele" behind her back, but then experimenting on humans was naturalized and she went on to win prizes.

As she walks, she sways from side to side and speaks. It's as though she needs to support herself with the words that leave her mouth without stopping. She gives him the same speech every time, tells him how difficult it is even in this day and age to be a woman and have a career, says that people continue to hold prejudices against her, that only recently have they started greeting her and not her assistant who's a man, because they think he's the one who's head of the laboratory, it was her choice not to have a family, and socially she has to pay for it, because people continue to think that women have to fulfil some biological plan, when her great accomplishment in life has been to press ahead, to never give in; being a man is so much easier, she says, this is her family—the laboratory—but no one understands, not really, she's revolutionizing medicine, she tells him, and people continue to care whether her shoes are feminine, or that her roots are showing because she didn't have time to go to the hairdresser, or that she's gained weight.

He agrees with everything she says, but he can't bear her words, which are like tiny tadpoles dragging themselves along, leaving behind a sticky trail, slithering until they pile up, one on top of the other, and rot, vitiating the air with their rancid smell. He doesn't answer because he also knows that she has few female employees working for her. And if one of them were to get pregnant, she'd look down on her, disregard her.

She shows him a cage and tells him that the specimen is a heroin addict. They've been supplying him with the drug for years to understand why addiction occurs. "When we nullify him, we'll study his brain," she says. Nullify, he thinks, another word that silences the horror.

Doctor Valka keeps talking, but again he's no longer listening. He sees specimens without eyes, others hooked up to tubes, breathing in nicotine all day long, other specimens have apparatuses on their heads, stuck to their skulls, some look like they're being starved, some have wires sticking out of every part of their body; he sees assistants performing vivisections, others pulling pieces of skin off the arms of specimens who haven't been given anaesthesia, and heads in cages that he knows have electrified floors. He thinks that the processing plant is better than this place, at least there death comes quickly.

They walk past a room with a specimen on a table. The specimen's chest has been cut open and his heart is beating. Several people stand around the table, studying him. Doctor Valka stops to look through the window. She says that it's wonderful to be able to record organ function when the specimen is alive and conscious. They gave him a mild sedative, she says, so he wouldn't faint from the pain. Excitedly she adds, "What a beautiful, beating heart! Isn't it incredible?"

He doesn't say anything.

"What was that?" she says.

"I didn't say anything," he tells her, but this time he looks her in the eye in a way that shows he's had enough and is impatient.

She regards him silently, her eyes moving from top to bottom, as though she were scanning him. It's a look intended to demonstrate her authority, but he ignores it. It's as though she doesn't know what to do with his indifference, and she takes him to a new room, one he's never been in. There are females in cages with their babies. They go up to a cage where a female appears to be dead and a baby that's two or three years old doesn't stop crying. She explains that they've sedated the mother to study the infant's reactions.

"What's the point? Isn't it obvious how the infant is going to react?" he asks her.

She doesn't answer and keeps walking, striking her cane against the floor, marking each step, containing her rage. She doesn't know how to react to his disinterest and he couldn't care less that she's growing impatient. The prospect of her complaining to Krieg doesn't bother him either. Better if she complains, he thinks, that way I can be sure I won't ever have to come back.

They walk past another room he can't recall having seen. But they don't go in. Through the windows, he sees animals in cages. He can make out dogs, rabbits, a few cats. "Are you trying to find a cure for the virus? I ask because you have animals in there. Isn't that dangerous?" he says to Valka.

"Everything we do here is confidential. That's why any visitor who sets foot in this laboratory signs a confidentiality agreement."

"Of course."

"I'm only interested in discussing experiments for which I require specimens you can obtain."

Doctor Valka never calls him by his name because she can't be bothered to memorize it. He suspects that the caged animals are a front. As long as someone is studying them and trying to find a cure, the virus is real.

"Isn't it strange that no one's found a cure? What with laboratories that are so advanced they're able to carry out cutting-edge experiments..."

The doctor doesn't look at him, or answer, but he feels that the little tadpoles in her throat are on the verge of bursting.

"I need strong specimens. Let me show you."

She takes him to a room on another floor where the specimens, all males, are sitting on seats similar to those found in cars. They've been immobilized and their heads are inside what look like square helmets made of metal bars. An assistant pushes a button and the helmet-like structure moves very fast, striking the specimen's head against a board that senses and registers the quantity, velocity and impact of the strikes. Some of the specimens appear to be dead because they don't react when the assistants try to wake them. Others look around disoriented, and have pained expressions on their faces. Valka says, "We simulate automobile accidents and collect data so that safer cars can be built. That's why we need more male specimens, strong ones, so that they can withstand several trials."

He knows that she expects him to say something about the wonderful work they're doing, work that could save lives, but the only thing he feels is the stone pressing against his chest.

An assistant approaches them and hands the doctor something to sign.

"What is this? Why am I only being asked to sign this now? Why didn't you give it to me earlier?"

"I did give it to you, Doctor, but you told me to come back later."

"That's not an acceptable answer. If I say later it means now, especially if it's something this important. I'm paying you to think. Now leave."

Though he's not looking at her, she says, "The incompetence of these people is beyond words."

He doesn't say anything because he thinks that working for this woman must be utterly maddening. What he would like to do is tell her that "later" means later and that when she insults her employees, she just comes across as a disloyal boss. But he thinks better of it, and says, "Incompetence? Aren't you the one who hires them, Doctor?"

She looks at him furiously.

He feels that the volcanic lava, cold and viscous, is on the verge of erupting. But she breathes deeply and says, "Please leave. I'll send the list directly to Krieg."

She says this like it's a threat, but he ignores her. There are so many more things he wants to tell her, but he says goodbye with a smile, puts his hands in his trouser pockets and turns around. He walks through the hallway whistling and hears the indignant strikes of her cane against the floor slowly grow distant.

16

He's getting into his car when Cecilia calls.

"Hi, Marcos. You're pixelated. Hello? Can you hear me? Can you see me?"

"Hi, Cecilia. Hello. Yes, I can hear you, but not well."

"Marc—"

The call cuts out. He drives for a while, pulls over, and then dials her number.

"Hi, Cecilia. The signal was bad back there."

"I heard about your father. Nelly called to tell me. How are you doing? Do you want some company?"

"I'm fine. Thanks, but I'd rather be alone."

"I understand. Are you having a farewell service?"

"Marisa's going to do it."

"Of course, that's to be expected. Do you want me to go?"

"No, but thanks. I don't even know if I'll go."

"I miss you, do you know that?"

He's silent. It's the first time she's said she misses him since she left.

She continues, "You look different, strange."

"I'm the same."

"It's just that for a while now you've seemed more distant."

"You don't want to come home. Do you expect me to spend my whole life waiting for you?"

"No, but it's just… I'd like us to talk."

"When I'm doing better, I'll call you, okay?"

She looks at him in the way she always has when she doesn't understand a situation or there's something that's beyond her. It's a look that's alert, but sad, a look like in an old sepia-coloured photograph.

"That's fine, whatever you prefer. Let me know if there's anything you need, Marcos."

"Okay. Take care."

When he gets home, he hugs Jasmine and whistles "Summertime" into her ear.

17

His sister has called countless times to organize the farewell service. She's clarified she'll take care of everything, "even the cost". When he heard her say this, he smiled at first, but then he was overcome by the feeling that he never wanted to see her again.

He wakes up early because he has to get into the city on time. Before he leaves, he showers with Jasmine to make sure she doesn't hurt herself. Then he gets her room ready, cleans it and fills the bowls with food and water so she'll be fine for a while. He checks her pulse and blood pressure. When he learnt she was pregnant, he put together a complete first-aid kit, picked up books on the subject, brought home a portable ultrasound machine, one of the ones they use at the plant to check impregnated females before they're sent to the game reserve. He trained himself to care for her and follow the stages of her pregnancy. Though he knows it's not ideal, it's the only option available to him because if he were to call a specialist, he'd have to register the pregnancy and provide documentation for the artificial insemination.

He puts on a suit and leaves.

While he's driving, his sister calls again.

"Marquitos, are you on your way? Why can't I see you?"

"I'm driving."

"Oh, okay. When will you be here?"

"I don't know."

"People are starting to arrive. I'd like to have the urn here, as you can imagine. Without the urn there's no point."

He hangs up without saying anything. She calls back, but he turns off his phone. Then he slows down. He'll take all the time he needs.

When he arrives at his sister's house, he sees a group of people going inside. They're carrying umbrellas. He gets out of the car, opens the boot and places the silver-plated urn under his arm. Then he rings the bell. His sister answers.

"Finally. Is something wrong with your phone? I couldn't call you back."

"I turned it off. Take the urn."

"Come in, come in, you don't have an umbrella again. Do you want to get yourself killed, Marcos?"

His sister says this and looks up at the sky. Then she takes the urn.

"Poor Dad. A life full of sacrifice. And in the end, we're nothing."

He looks at his sister and thinks there's something strange about her. Then he looks more closely and realizes she's wearing make-up, has been to the hairdresser and has on a tight black dress. None of it's over the top, so as not to show a complete lack of respect, but she's sufficiently put together to look good at what is without a doubt her event.

"Come in. Help yourself to whatever you like."

When he goes into the dining room, he sees that the guests have gathered around the table. It's been pushed up against the wall and different dishes have been placed on it so people can serve themselves. His sister carries the urn to a smaller table where there's a transparent box that looks to be made of etched glass. She places the urn inside the box carefully, with a degree of grandiloquence so people can see how much she respects her father. Next to the box is an electronic picture frame with images of him changing on the screen, a vase of flowers and a basket full of party favours with his photo and the date of his birth and death on them. The photos have been retouched. He can't recall there being any shots of his father with his sister and her family, or hugging her kids, because they never went to see him at the nursing home. In another photo, his sister and father are at the zoo. He remembers that day, his sister was a baby. She's erased him from the photo and inserted herself into it. People approach her and offer their condolences. She takes out a handkerchief and raises it to her tearless eyes.

He doesn't know anyone. And he's not hungry. He sits down in an armchair and looks at the people in the room. He sees his niece and nephew in a corner, dressed in black, looking at their phones. They see him but don't greet him. He doesn't feel like getting up to talk to them either. People look bored. They eat things from the table, talk quietly. He hears a tall man in a suit who looks like he might be a lawyer or an accountant, say to another guest, "The price of meat has really dropped recently. Special beef goes for a lot less than it did two months ago. I read this article that said the drop in prices has to do with the fact that India's officially decided to sell and export special meat. It was prohibited before and now they're selling it for hardly anything."

The man he's talking to, who's bald and has a forgettable face, laughs and says, "Well, yeah, there are millions of them. Wait till people start eating them and then the prices will stabilize." An older woman stops in front of his father's urn and looks at the photos. She picks up one of the party favours and inspects it. She smells it and then tosses it back into the basket. The woman sees a cockroach on the wall. It's crawling very close to the electronic picture frame where the fake photos of his father continue to change on the screen. She panics, steps back and leaves. The cockroach crawls into the basket of party favours.

Except for him, there isn't a single person in the place who knows his father was captivated by birds, that he was passionately in love with his wife and when she died, something in him went out for good.

His sister walks back and forth with short, quick steps, taking care of the guests. He hears her talking to someone and say, "It's based on the technique of death by a thousand cuts. That's right, it's from that book that just came out. The best-seller. I have no idea, my husband's the one who takes care of it." What could his sister possibly know about a form of Chinese torture? He stands up and moves closer so he can keep listening, but she heads to the kitchen. When he goes over to the food table, he sees a silver platter containing an arm that's being filleted. He doesn't doubt that the arm is oven roasted. It's surrounded by lettuce and radishes that have been cut to resemble tiny lotus flowers. The guests try the arm and say, "It's exquisite, really fresh. Marisa's such a great hostess. You can tell how much she loved her father." Then he remembers the cold room.

He goes towards the kitchen, but in the hallway he runs into his sister.

"Where are you going, Marquitos?"

"To the kitchen."

"Why are you going to the kitchen? I'll get you anything you need."

He doesn't answer and keeps walking. She grabs him by the arm, but then lets go because the person who was calling her from the dining room has just come up to her to talk.

When he reaches the kitchen, it's as if he's been struck by a smell that's rancid, if fleeting. He walks towards the door to the cold room. He looks inside and sees a head without an arm. "So she got herself a female, that skank," he thinks. Domestic heads are a status symbol in the city; they give a household prestige. He looks at the head more closely and when he makes out a few sets of initials, he realizes she's an FGP. Off to the side on the countertop, he sees a book. His sister doesn't have books. The book's title is *Domestic Heads: Your Guide to Death by a Thousand Cuts*. There are red and brown stains in the book. He feels he might vomit. Of course, he thinks, she's going to carve the head up slowly, serving pieces every time she hosts an event. The death by a thousand cuts thing must be some sort of trend if all her guests are talking about it. An activity for the whole family, cutting up the living being in the fridge, based on a thousand-year-old form of Chinese torture. The domestic head looks at him sadly. He tries to open the door, but it's locked.

"What are you doing?"

His sister has returned, holding an empty platter in her hands and taps the floor with her right foot. He turns around and sees her there. That's when he feels the stone in his chest shatter.

"You disgust me."

She looks at him, her expression between shocked and indignant.

"How can you say that to me, today of all days. And what's been going on with you lately? You've had this preoccupied look on your face."

"What's been going on with me is that you're a hypocrite and your children are two little shits."

He shocks himself with the insult. She opens her eyes and mouth, and for a few seconds doesn't say anything.

"I understand you're stressed because of Dad, but you can't insult me like that, you're in my house."

"Can't you see you're incapable of thinking for yourself? The only thing you do is follow the norms imposed on you. Can't you see that this whole thing is a superficial act? Are you even capable of feeling something, really feeling it? I mean, have you ever cared about Dad?"

"I think a farewell service was called for, don't you? It's the least we could do for him."

"You don't understand anything."

He walks out of the kitchen and she follows behind, saying he can't leave, what will people think, he can't take the urn now, he could at least give her this, the house is full of Esteban's colleagues and his boss is here, her own brother can't embarrass her like this. He stops, grabs her by the arm and says into her ear, "If you keep fucking with me, I'll tell everyone how you did nothing when it came to Dad, understood?" His sister looks at him in fear and takes a few steps back.

He opens the front door and leaves. She runs after him with the urn and reaches the car just before he gets in.

"Take the urn, Marquitos."

For a few seconds, he looks at her in silence. Then he gets into the car and closes the door. His sister stands there not knowing what to do until she realizes she's outdoors and doesn't have an umbrella. She looks up at the sky in fear, covers her head with her hand and runs into the house.

He starts the car and drives away, but first he watches his sister enter the house holding an urn full of dirty sand from an abandoned zoo with no name.

18

He accelerates and heads home, turns on the radio.

That's when his phone rings. It's Mari. The call strikes him as odd because she knows he's at his father's farewell service. Mari knows this because she phoned to ask for permission to give his contacts to his sister, who wanted to invite them to the service. He of course said no and told Mari he didn't want to see anyone he knew.

"Hi, Mari. What's going on?"

"I need you to come to the plant now. I know it's not the best timing, I apologize, but we've got a situation here that we can't handle. I'm asking you to please come now."

"Hold on, what happened?"

"I can't explain, you'll have to come see for yourself."

"I'm not far, I was on my way home. I'll be there in ten minutes."

He accelerates, thinks he's never heard Mari sound so worried.

When he nears the plant, he sees what looks like a trailer truck in the distance. It's stopped in the middle of the highway. When he's a few metres away, he sees bloodstains on the pavement. When he gets closer still, he can't believe his eyes.

A cage trailer has overturned on the side of the highway and been destroyed. The doors either got smashed on impact or were torn off. He sees Scavengers with machetes, sticks, knives, ropes, killing the heads that were being transported to the processing plant. He sees desperation and hunger, rabid madness and ingrained resentment, he sees murder, he sees a Scavenger cutting the arm off a live head, he sees another Scavenger running and trying to lasso an escaping head as though he were a calf, he sees women with babies on their backs wielding machetes, cutting off limbs, hands, feet, he sees the pavement covered in guts, he sees a boy who's five or six dragging an arm. He accelerates when a Scavenger, his face wild and splattered with blood, yells something at him and raises a machete.

He feels the shards of stone in his chest move through his body. They burn, they're candescent.

When he arrives, Mari, Krieg and several employees are outside the plant, watching the spectacle. Mari runs over and hugs him.

"I'm sorry, Marcos, I'm so sorry, but this is insane. Nothing like this has ever happened with the Scavengers."

"Did the truck overturn on its own or did they do it?"

"We don't know. But that isn't the worst part."

"What's the worst part, Mari, what could be worse than this?"

"They attacked Luisito, the driver. He was injured and couldn't get out in time. They killed him, Marcos, they killed him."

Mari hugs him and doesn't stop crying.

Krieg comes over and holds out his hand. "I'm sorry about your father. I apologize for calling you in like this."

"It was the right thing to do."

"Those degenerates killed Luisito."

"The police will have to be called."

"We'll get to that. What we need to do now is find a way to stop those fuckers."

"They have enough meat for weeks, if they want."

"I told the workers to fire but not kill them, to scare them off."

"And what happened?"

"Nothing. It's like they're in a trance. Like they've become these savage monsters."

"Let's talk in your office. But I'll get some tea for Mari first."

They go into the plant. He hugs Mari, who can't stop crying and says that of all the drivers, Luisito was one of her favourites, that he was a good kid, not even thirty and so responsible, the father of a family, of a beautiful baby boy, and what about his wife, what was she going to do now, life's not fair, Mari says, the Scavengers are filth, scum that should have been killed long ago, fuckers who are always lurking around like cockroaches, they're not humans, she says, they're degenerates, wild animals, and dying like Luisito did is an atrocity, his wife won't be able to cremate her own husband, and how come no one saw this coming, she says, all of them are at fault, and which god should she pray to if her god lets things like this happen.

He sits her down and gets her a cup of tea. She seems to compose herself a little and touches his hand.

"How are you holding up, Marcos? You seem different, more tired than usual. For a while now. Are you sleeping okay?"

"I am, Mari, thanks."

"Your dad was a wonderful person. So honest. Have I ever told you that I knew him before the Transition?"

She has told him, many times, but he says she hasn't and looks surprised, like he does every time.

"It was when I was young. I worked as a secretary at a tannery and I spoke to him whenever he came in for meetings with my old boss."

And then she tells him again that his father was very charming, "Like you, Marcos," she says, and that all the women at the tannery had their eyes on him, but that he never did anything, not even look at them. "Because you could tell your dad only had eyes for your mum, you could see he was in love," she says. He was always so pleasant and respectful, you could tell from a mile away that he was a good person.

He takes Mari's hands carefully and kisses them.

"Thank you, Mari. You're looking a little better, do you mind if I go talk to Krieg?"

"Go ahead, love, this needs to be dealt with, it's urgent."

"I'm here if you need anything."

Mari stands up and she plants a kiss on his cheek and hugs him.

He goes into Krieg's office and sits down.

"This is a disaster," Krieg says. "The heads amount to a huge loss, but what happened to Luisito is horrific."

"Yeah, we have to call his wife."

"The police will take care of that. They'll let her know in person."

"Do we know what happened? Did the truck overturn on its own or was it the Scavengers?"

"We have to go over the security footage, but we believe the Scavengers are responsible. There was no reaction time."

"Was it Oscar who let you know?"

"Yes, Oscar is on duty. He saw the truck and called me. Not five minutes had passed before those shits were killing them all."

"So it was planned."

"That seems to be the case."

"They'll do it again now that they know it's possible."

"I know, that's what I'm afraid of. What do you think we should do?"

He doesn't know what to say, or rather he knows perfectly well what to say, but doesn't want to. The pieces of stone blaze in his blood. He thinks of the boy dragging the arm along the pavement. He's silent. Krieg looks at him anxiously.

When he tries to say something, he coughs. He feels the pieces of stone accumulate in his throat. They're burning it. He wishes he could escape with Jasmine. He wishes he could disappear.

"The only thing I can think to do is go over there now and kill them all. That's what needs to be done with degenerates, they need to be disappeared," Krieg says.

He looks at Krieg and feels a sadness that's contaminated, furious. He can't stop coughing. He feels the pieces of stone break down into grains of sand in his throat. Krieg hands him a glass of water.

"Are you okay?"

He wants to tell Krieg that he's not okay, that the stones are scorching his insides, that he can't get the boy who was dying of hunger out of his mind. He takes a sip of water, he doesn't want to respond, but does, "What we'll have to do is get some heads, poison them and give them to the Scavengers."

Doubtful about how to proceed, he's silent again, but then continues, "I'll give the order in a few weeks. We'll have to wait until they eat the meat they stole and don't suspect anything. It would be strange if we gave them some heads now, right after they've attacked us."

Krieg looks at him nervously, thinks it over for a few seconds, and then smiles. "It's a good idea."

"This way when they're poisoned to death, people will think it was the meat they stole. No one will accuse us."

"It'll have to be done by people who can be trusted."

"I'll take care of it when the time comes."

"But the police will be here soon, they'll likely arrest them. I don't think it'll be necessary."

He detests being this efficient. But he doesn't stop answering, resolving problems, trying to find the best option for the plant.

"Who are they going to arrest? Over a hundred people living deprived, marginal lives? How will they know who killed Luisito, who to blame? If it shows up in the security footage, that's one thing, but it'll be a long time before that happens."

"You're right. Say they arrest two or three of them, we'll still have problems with the others. But how many heads do we need to kill them all?"

"Not all of them, we'll kill enough for the rest to leave."

"Right."

"These people exist outside the law. It's unlikely they even have IDs. We could be talking years for the investigation, and in the interim, they'll overturn more trucks because now they know how to do it."

"Tomorrow I'll have armed staff on duty for the trucks' arrival."

"That too. Though I don't think they'll risk it."

"You didn't see the wild look on their faces."

"I did. But they'll be tired and fed. Though I do agree it's a good idea to have armed staff now."

"Good. I trust this is going to work."

He doesn't say anything, just shakes Krieg's hand and says he's going home. Krieg says okay, that he should absolutely go home, and apologizes for having called him at a time like this.

As he drives away from the plant, he sees the destroyed truck again, the blue lights of the police cars approaching, the blood on the pavement.

He wants to pity the Scavengers and be sorry about Luisito's fate, but he doesn't feel a thing.

19

He gets home and goes straight to Jasmine's room. He hasn't looked at his phone once to see if she's okay. It's the first time since he installed the cameras that he's forgotten to check on her.

When he opens the door, he sees that Jasmine is lying down and looks to be in pain. She's touching her belly and her nightgown is stained. He runs up to her and sees that the mattress is soaked with a brownish-green fluid. "No!" he yells.

He knows, because of all he's read, that if the amniotic fluid is green or brown, there's a problem with the baby. He doesn't know what to do other than pick Jasmine up and take her to his bed so she's more comfortable. Then he grabs his phone and calls Cecilia.

"I need you to come over now."

"Marcos?"

"Get in your mum's car and drive here."

"But Marcos, what's going on?"

"Just come over now, Cecilia. I need you here now."

"But I don't understand. You sound different, I don't recognize you."

"I can't explain over the phone, just know that I need you to come now."

"Okay, I'm on my way."

He knows she'll be a while. Her mother's house isn't in the city, but it's not close either.

When he hangs up, he runs to the kitchen, grabs some dish towels and wets them. He puts the cold cloth to Jasmine's forehead. Then he tries to give her an ultrasound, but he doesn't detect a problem. He touches her belly and says, "Everything's gonna be just fine, little one, just fine, your birth's gonna go well, everything's gonna be just fine." He gives Jasmine some water. Over and over he says these words, he can't stop, though he knows his child might die. He can't bring himself to get up and take care of the things that need to be done for labour, like boil water. Instead, he doesn't move and clings to Jasmine, who's becoming paler by the minute.

He looks at the print hanging above his bed, at the Chagall his mother loved so much. It's then that he prays, in a way. He asks his mother for help, wherever she is.

That's when he hears a car engine and runs outside. He hugs Cecilia. She steps back and looks at him with surprise. He puts his hand on her arm, but before he takes her inside, he says, "I need you to have an open mind. I need you to set aside whatever you might feel and be the professional nurse I know."

"I don't know what you're talking about, Marcos."

"Come and I'll show you. Please help me."

When they enter the room, Cecilia sees a woman lying on the bed, pregnant. Cecilia looks at him with sadness in her eyes, and a bit of surprise, and confusion. But then she moves closer and sees the mark on the woman's forehead.

"Why is there a female in my bed? Why didn't you call a specialist?"

"The baby is mine."

She looks at him with disgust. Then she takes a few steps back, crouches down and puts her head between her hands, as though her blood pressure has dropped.

"Are you crazy? Do you want to end up in the Municipal Slaughterhouse? How could you have been with a female? You're sick."

He goes to her, slowly lifts her to her feet and hugs her. Then he says, "The amniotic fluid is green, Cecilia, the baby's going to die."

As though his words were magical, she begins to move and tells him to start boiling water, to bring clean towels, alcohol, more pillows. He runs through the house looking for these things while she examines Jasmine and tries to calm her down.

The labour lasts several hours. Jasmine pushes instinctively, but Cecilia can't make herself understood. He tries to help, but feels Jasmine's fear and it paralyses him. All he can do is say, "It's gonna be fine, everything's gonna be just fine," until Cecilia shouts that she can see a foot. He panics. Cecilia tells him to leave, she says he's making both her and Jasmine nervous, and that the birth could be complicated. She tells him to wait outside.

He waits behind the door to the room, his ear pressed against the wood. There are no shouts, just Cecilia's voice saying, "Come on, honey, push, push, that's it, come on, you can do this, harder, it's on its way now, come on, love, that's it, that's it," as though Jasmine could understand her. Then there's complete silence. The minutes pass and he hears Cecilia yell, "No! Come on, little one, turn around, come on, honey, push, come on, it's almost there, almost there.

Please God, help me. You are not going to die on me, no fucking way, not while I'm here. Come on, love, that's it, you can do this." For a few minutes he doesn't hear anything, and then he hears a cry, and goes in.

His child is in Cecilia's arms. She's covered in sweat, her hair is a mess, but she's smiling, and it lights up her face.

"It's a boy."

He goes up to her and takes the baby in his arms, rocks him, kisses him. The baby cries. Cecilia says that the umbilical cord needs to be cut, and the baby cleaned and wrapped up. She says this between tears, she's emotional, happy.

Once she's taken care of these things, Cecilia hands back the baby, who's now calmed down. He looks at his son in disbelief. "He's beautiful," he says, "he's just beautiful." He feels the shards of stone shrink, lose their hold.

Jasmine is in bed and she stretches out her arms. They ignore her, but she opens her mouth and moves her hands. She tries to get up, and then she does, and bumps into the night table with her hips, and knocks over the lamp.

They look at her silently.

"Go get some more towels and water to clean her before you take her out to the barn," Cecilia tells him.

He gets up and gives his son to Cecilia, who begins to rock and sing to him. "He's ours now," he tells her, and she looks at him, unable to respond, emotional, confused.

All Cecilia can do is look at the baby and cry silently. She cuddles him and says, "What a beautiful baby, you're the most adorable baby boy. What are we going to call you?"

He goes to the kitchen and returns with something in his right hand.

Jasmine is only able to stretch out her arms desperately towards her son. She tries to get up again but is cut by the pieces of glass from the broken lamp.

He sits down behind Jasmine. She looks back at him in despair. First he puts his arms around her and kisses the mark on her forehead. He tries to calm her down. Then he gets onto his knees on the floor, and says, "Easy does it, everything's gonna be just fine, take it easy." With a wet rag he wipes the sweat from her forehead. He sings "Summertime" into her ear.

When she calms down a little, he stands up and grabs her by the hair. Jasmine is only able to move her hands, is trying to reach her son. She wants to speak, to scream, but there are no sounds. He picks up the club he brought from the kitchen and hits her on the forehead, right where she's been branded. Jasmine falls to the floor, stunned, unconscious.

Cecilia jumps when she hears the thud and looks at him without understanding. "Why?" she yells. "She could have given us more children."

As he drags the body of the female to the barn to slaughter it, he says to Cecilia, his voice radiant, so pure it wounds: "She had the human look of a domesticated animal."

AFTERWORD

THE MANY LIVES OF *TENDER IS THE FLESH*

In 2018, a woman reported me to the Argentine Society of Writers (SADE). She informed me in a Facebook post, which she had tagged me in. The reason? She was indignant about the ending of *Tender is the Flesh.* She didn't understand how the author, a feminist, could have written something so misogynistic. Let's rewind. A woman buys *Tender is the Flesh,* she reads it, finishes it, becomes enraged. I envision her in pyjamas, pacing around her house, talking to herself, yelling into the void, perhaps slamming a door, and wailing, How could Bazterrica have written THAT ENDING? Then she takes a deep breath, gets dressed very slowly, brushes her hair, applies a touch of makeup to conceal her furious expression, opens the door angrily, and drops her keys in her purse, carelessly, because she's thinking about everything she's going to say when she reaches her destination. She takes a taxi or a bus, or maybe she walks to the nearest SADE office to report my novel. I imagine the look on the face of the person she speaks to. I imagine them trying to contain their laughter, or their surprise, or frankly, their urge to kick out this woman who wants... what? To change the ending of a book that's already been published? To have it removed from bookstores? Burnt? For me to take back what I wrote? What she really wants, I sense, is for someone to be indignant alongside her, a person with whom she can share everything she felt about the damn book. That's glorious, isn't it? It really is. It's one of the biggest compliments I've received in my life. In fact, I told my publisher that we should put a promotional banner on the book saying "Clarín Prize 2017 / Reported to the SADE 2018".

Many people had a similar response to the SADE Woman, and I think that explains why the book has been translated into over thirty languages and read by thousands (I'd venture to say millions) of people, why it's taught in schools across Argentina and continues to be read today. People have fainted, others have felt nauseous, or had nightmares; they've returned their copies to bookstores, horrified, they've accused me of being a cannibal, depraved, violent, a murderer. For a book to do all this, for it to unsettle, disturb, cause—as one woman told me—readers to taste blood in their mouths, is truly a marvel. I think the worst possible response to a book I've written would be complete indifference. That's why I'm in a state of total gratitude when it comes to *Tender is the Flesh.* What a privilege it is to be read today, having published this novel so many years ago; what a miracle to be read by other cultures, by teenagers who confess it's the first book they've finished, by people who don't usually read.

This book has also made possible beautiful, moving experiences that have brought me to tears. In 2024, I spoke at an adult learning centre. The students hadn't finished secondary school and wanted to do so as adults. There was one woman who held her small daughter in her arms. She struggled to talk to me. She told me that *Tender is the Flesh* had been the first book she'd read. It was all I could do not to cry in front of her. I was moved because I know that structural inequality means many people don't have the time or energy or money to read. Reading is a luxury. I was incredibly proud that she had finished the book. I think that's worth more than any prize. In 2025, in Medellín, Colombia, a reader told me that *Tender is the Flesh* had helped him change degrees at university. He had been enrolled in a programme that centred on animal cruelty, he was disgusted and sad, but it was only after reading my book that he decided to study biology, and now he was happy. In 2024, in Panama, one reader attended the launch with the Argentine cover airbrushed onto her nails. I asked her on stage to show them to the audience. They applauded. Afterwards, she stayed behind to talk and another reader approached us and joined our conversation. Today, they're a couple, and they met thanks to her *Tender is the Flesh* nails. In 2025, in Buenos Aires, a woman told me that *Tender is the Flesh* had reconnected her with her fifteen-year-old granddaughter. They had formed a bond after reading the book together, and they have continued to do so with other books. I can tell many such stories. Students have put on plays of the novel and dressed up as characters when I've visited their schools. They've given me works of art, mugs, shirts, written alternative endings (Mrs. SADE would be very pleased), made book trailers, interactive games (one of which I played—I came in third!!), composed songs, poems, and essays with in-depth analyses, and organized *Tender is the Flesh* themed events, and this is at all kinds of schools. To date, I've spoken at over a hundred.

But let's rewind once again. Did I think all this was going to happen when I wrote the book? Definitely not. As I wrote, I just asked myself: Is this story working? Does it hold together? Is this word precise? The novel is dedicated to my brother, Gonzalo Bazterrica, who's a chef, and at his restaurant, he and I have spent hours talking about conscious eating. Hippocrates summarized conscious eating in a single sentence: "Let food be thy medicine and medicine be thy food." During the process of researching and reading about the subject, I changed my diet and stopped eating meat in Argentina. I repeat: I stopped eating meat in Argentina, where barbecues are practically sacred rituals. And something remarkable happened, which is that I denaturalized the consumption of meat and began to see a slab of steak on a plate as a piece of carcass. I thought: "We're animals, we're made of meat, we could easily be hung from a hook in a butcher shop next to a cow's carcass." After that, I spent six months researching without writing a word. I researched slaughterhouse operations, rights of non-human animals and cannibalism. I read numerous essays, instruction manuals, works of fiction, and watched a lot of movies, documentaries and institutional videos from slaughterhouses. I'm often asked how many horror books or dystopias I read before writing *Tender is the Flesh* and the truth is almost none, because I don't think of literature as being fragmented into genres; instead, everything is literature for me, and to write, I nourish myself as much with a poem as I do with an essay or documentary.

A few years ago, a woman sent me a podcast in which two readers from the United States discussed *Tender is the Flesh*. They'd liked it, but felt it was implausible, that the government would never take away your animals and kill them due to a supposed virus. Right, I thought, these people have never lived in Latin America. In my country, during the civic-military-ecclesiastical dictatorship, the government kidnapped your loved ones, tortured them, killed them and disappeared their bodies. Therefore, the government could take away your animals. I published *Tender is the Flesh* in 2017, and there's a scene that takes place at a game reserve, only the animal being hunted is a human. In 2025, we learned that millionaire snipers spent their weekends killing civilians during the Siege of Sarajevo. They did this for fun. It happened. It was real. As I write this, in 2026, none of these killers have been caught. The slaughter was permitted by people with power, people who concealed the identities of the millionaire killers and who continue to do so, as none of their names have been published. Did I know this about the Siege of Sarajevo when I wrote *Tender is the Flesh*? I didn't, but I did know human beings are capable of such horror and a good deal more. In the novel, I examined and reflected on the cannibalistic impulse of the world, on how human beings are capable of naturalizing and justifying so many horrors. We are devourers of otherness. When it comes to non-human animals, we place ourselves in a very arrogant position as a species, but bees are the only species that are truly essential; without bees, everything would collapse. We pollute, we have an extractivist mindset when it comes to nature, regarding it as separate from us, but we don't realize that we're the air we breathe, the water we drink, the nature we're destroying. We humans also cannibalize one another by constructing categories of class; this is not real, but it allows those considered elite or superior to consume others, symbolically and literally, without consequence.

Despite having written *Tender is the Flesh*, I do believe in humanity. Even though predation, cruelty and a celebration of ignorance predominate in the world today, there are also people who devote their lives to helping others, animals and nature, people who have a spirit of abundance, of building together, of illuminating the matrix we live in, of making it a little less cruel. *Tender is the Flesh* opened many doors for me. It has given me and continues to give me singular life experiences, it has allowed me to travel, to meet a myriad of people, to connect with other writers, and ultimately, to earn a living from my books, to discuss literature, to spend each of my days working on what I love—that is, to live the dream. For this reason, I want to thank my readers very much. Thank you for reading *Tender is the Flesh* and for recommending it, even if you hate me because of the ending, or the puppies, or because you think I'm a crazy cannibal (which I'm not—or am I?). Even if you come to Argentina just to report me to the SADE (wouldn't that be glorious?), I'll always be grateful to you. Thank you, thank you, thank you.

AGUSTINA BAZTERRICA, FEBRUARY 2026
TRANSLATED BY SARAH MOSES

ACKNOWLEDGEMENTS

To Liliana Díaz Mindmurry, Félix Bruzzone, Gabriela Cabezón Cámara, Pilar Bazterrica, Ricardo Uzal García, Camila Bazterrica Uzal, Lucas Bazterrica Uzal, Juan Cruz Bazterrica, Daniela Benítez, Antonia Bazterrica, Gaspar Bazterrica, Fermín Bazterrica, Fernanda Navas, Rita Piacentini, Bemi Fiszbein, Pamela Terlizzi Prina, Alejandra Keller, Laura Lina, Mónica Piazza, Agustina Caride, Valeria Correa Fiz, Mavi Saracho, Nicolás Hochman, Gonzalo Gálvez Romano, Diego Tomasi, Alan Ojeda, Marcos Urdapilleta, Valentino Cappelloni, Juan Otero, Julían Pigna, Alejo Miranda, Bernadita Crespo, Ramiro Altamirano, Vivi Valdés.

To my parents, Mercedes Jones and Jorge Bazterrica.

To Mariano Borobio, always.

PUSHKIN PRESS

TENDER IS THE FLESH

'Horribly effective… This provocative novel expertly wields a double-edged cleaver… "in the end, meat is meat, it doesn't matter where it's from", it's a statement of both dystopic extremity and banal everyday fact'

Guardian

'Bazterrica's writing is ferocious; she has vision and intent. When you least expect it, her narrative hits her target, and leaves you trembling'

Samanta Schweblin, author of *Good and Evil and Other Stories*

'Sitting comfortably? Not after even the tiniest nibble of this gut-churning, brilliantly realised novel'

Daily Mail

'A compelling dystopian novel'

Independent

'Chilling… [a] very contemporary parable'

Observer

'Told with a chilly aloofness that makes the horror of it all the more disturbing'

Financial Times

'A skin-crawling yet compelling read'

Refinery29

'Unflinching until the end, with a disturbing finale that leaves you as dazed as one of the poor specimens in the abattoir'

Culturefly

Agustina Bazterrica is an Argentinian novelist and short-story writer. She is a central figure in the Buenos Aires literary scene, working as a cultural organiser and workshop curator. She has received several awards for her writing, most notably the Premio Clarín Novela for *Tender is the Flesh*, which has been translated into over 20 languages. Her collection of short stories, *Nineteen Claws and a Black Bird*, and her third novel, *The Unworthy*, are also available from Pushkin Press.

Sarah Moses is a Canadian writer and translator of French and Spanish. She has translated work by Tomás Downey and Ariana Harwicz, whose novel *Die, My Love* was longlisted for the International Booker Prize, among other awards. Her collection of short fiction, *Strange Water*, was published in 2024.